FIZZLEBERT STUMP

THE

BOY WHO CRIED FISH

A.F. HARROLD

ILLUSTRATED BY
SARAH HORNE

BLOOMSBURY

NEW YORK LONDON NEW DELHI SYDNEY

for Dan & Jo

Bloomsbury Publishing, London, New Delhi, New York and Sydney

First published in Great Britain in 2014 by Bloomsbury Publishing Plc

50 Bedford Square, London WC1B 3DP

Copyright© A.F. Harrold 2014
Illustrations copyright © Sarah Horne

The moral right of the author and illustrator has been asserted.

A CIP catalogue record for this book is available from the British Library

ISBN 978 1 4088 4246 1

FIZZLEBERT STUMP

THE

BOY WHO CRIED FISH

SOME THINGS PEOPLE SAID ABOUT THE FIZZLEBERT STUMP BOOKS

Wonderfully told, fabulously eccentric, and certain to leave everyone in the family wearing a broad smile.

— Jeremy Strong

Fantastically funny

— Primary Teacher

Walks a high-wire of daft ideas and deft storytelling, ringmastered by a narrator who intrudes on the action with hilariously incongruous asides. Top fun at the Big Top.

— Financial Times

One of the funniest books I've ever read!
— Amy, 10, Girl Talk

If you like funny, exciting and entertaining books, read about Fizzlebert Stump. The author keeps the reader gripped by the way he ends each chapter, making you want to read on to find out what happens next. Even my mum enjoyed this book and I had to keep telling her what was happening!
— Freya Hudson, 10, Lovereading4kids

CHAPTER ONE

In which introductions are made and in which a stranger is spotted

This is a book about fish, and it's a book about Fish, but mostly it's a book about a boy. If you looked at the front cover you'll probably already know this since it's got a boy's name written across the top in big letters, and the biggest words on the front of a book are always the most important ones (or the shortest ones, because it's difficult to make short ones fill the space properly without making them big). But instead of going on about the cover we ought to pay some attention to the insides of the book, which is, after all, what you're reading now. So, here we go . . .

Fizzlebert, who some people call Fizz for short (or Fizzlebert Stump for long (or Young Mr Fizzlebert Stump for even longer (or Fizzlebert Graham Stump for embarrassing purposes))), was sitting on the steps outside his caravan sipping a cup of hot chocolate.

It was late in the evening. Overhead a few stars valiantly pushed their way through a smattering of clouds. The distant noise of a crowd of perfectly normal people going home could be heard off in the distance, round the other side of the Big Top, and Fizz was smiling to himself (between sips) at the memory of a job well done.

In the circus it was always important to put on a good show. The best publicity, they say, is word of mouth, and if your audience see a lacklustre show they'll go to work or to school the next morning and tell their friends, 'Well, it was *okay*, I mean, if you like unfunny clowns, a weak strongman, missing sequins and an out-of-tune sea lion.' If you heard a review like that, would you want to go and visit the circus the next night? And a circus always needed people to go the next night (unless they were due a day off. Which this evening they weren't.).

Fizz was certain that he hadn't let anyone down. His act, with Charles the lion and Captain Fox-Dingle the lion-tamer (although

Charles was so friendly he hadn't needed taming for years), had been a star turn. He'd put his head in the lion's mouth even further than normal and had held it in for very nearly a whole minute, which, considering the smell, was not to be sniffed at. And then, when Captain Fox-Dingle had tapped him on the shoulder and he'd pulled his head out, he'd done so with such grace and aplomb, in such a swift, deft movement, that the applause was guaranteed. It was something people would be telling their friends at work or in the playground about the next day for sure. And for all the right reasons.

Fizz was especially pleased because recently the act hadn't gone quite so smoothly. Charles sometimes let his mouth droop a bit and once or twice Fizz had caught his ear or his cheek on

 4

a tooth as he withdrew his head. Fortunately Charles always wore his false teeth, the ones made from rubber, so no harm had been done, but it had made it a bit awkward, less slick than was professional, and he'd seen the Ringmaster give them A Look.

The Ringmaster is the master of the circus, and A Look from him isn't something to be ignored. It means, 'Tut tut,' and any act that gets one of those knows that socks need pulling up. If an act ever gets too sloppy then the Ringmaster doesn't give the act A Look, but A Word. Fizz had never had A Word, and he didn't want one now, which was why he was smiling at how well the show had gone, especially after that afternoon's rehearsal.

They'd just been going through the act (it never hurts to practise) and while Fizz had his

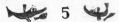

head in the lion's mouth, Charles did something he'd never done before. He fell asleep.

The great wet rubbery teeth fell shut around Fizz's head. For a moment he was stuck but by pushing on Charles's nose he managed to pull free. It was only when he tried to stand up straight that he realised he was wearing Charles's false teeth like a crown. A wet white toothy crown that covered his face, but a crown all the same.

Fizz had looked at Charles, all gummy and shut-eyed, snoring away (while still sat up) and he'd shuddered. Captain Fox-Dingle had shuddered beside him.

They both knew that if such a thing happened in a real show, with an audience watching, it would be the funniest thing that the spectators had ever seen. This would be great if they were clowns, but a lion tamer and his proud king-of-the-jungle companion are not a comedy act. In fact, there's nothing sadder, nothing more embarrassing, nothing more depressing than a toothless lion who's being pointed at and laughed at by five hundred strangers.

But that had been at rehearsal. The show, as I've mentioned several times already, had gone without a hitch and Fizz was sitting out in the fresh air, smiling to himself and drinking his hot chocolate when he saw the bobbing beard of the bearded boy, Wystan Barboozul, running towards him through the gloom of the evening.

'Fizz!'

Wystan (an orphan the circus had picked up in an earlier book) was a boy about Fizz's age who did an acrobatic act with Fish the sea lion which was *almost* as good as the act Fizz did with Charles the land lion. He was a somewhat grumpy boy normally, given to complaining and beard-stroking silences, never mean, but then again not often jolly either. The fact he was running up shouting in an excited manner caught Fizz's attention.

'Wystan? What is it?' he asked as the

bearded boy leant on his knees and got his breath back.

'Oh, Fizz,' he said between pants (Fizzlebert's mum had hung the washing out to dry that afternoon and hadn't taken it in yet. Wystan didn't seem to notice the underwear hanging either side of his head (one pair said 'Monday' and the other said '14th of April' and both had Fizzlebert's dad's name sewn in the back of them).). 'I just saw something really weird.'

'What was it?' Fizz asked.

I ought to tell you one thing, before letting Wystan speak. While Fizzlebert had been doing *his* daring act with Charles and the Captain, and while everyone else had been doing *their* daring acts in the ring, the bearded boy had not been doing anything daring at all. His act with Fish, the sea lion, had been cancelled. They hadn't done it. None of it.

To explain why we need a quick flashback to earlier on that evening. Here goes. (In a television show they often do flashbacks in black and white, to make it look different to the bits of the show that are happening here and now. The problem I have is that this whole book is in black and white, so you'll just have to imagine that this next bit's *even more* black and white than the rest of it. Trust me, I'm an author.)

The two boys were having their tea in the mess tent. Fizz was pushing the fricasséed clown fish round in its sauce (it didn't seem quite right to be eating it, not when his mum was a clown human), and watching an argument.

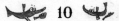

10

By the serving station, where Cook ladled out portions of food, the Ringmaster was looking at the steaming mound of dinner that had just landed on his plate.

'Fish again?' he asked.

'Yes, fish again,' snapped Cook.

'Mmm,' said the Ringmaster, in a way that suggested he wasn't that fond of fish.

'We *are* parked by the seaside, Ringmaster. Plenty of fish around.'

'Well, maybe tomorrow we could have some vegetables as well?'

Cook threw a hand in the air (though not very high since it was still attached to his wrist) and made a huffing noise.

'I'll have a word with me suppliers,' he grumbled.

Cook was a wiry man, with heavy stubble

and red, bloodshot eyes. In years gone by he would've had a cigarette hanging from his bottom lip, but in these health-conscious days he didn't. He'd replaced it with a stubby little pencil, which didn't burn as well, but gave him something to wiggle between his lips and was much more useful for making notes on recipes.

The Ringmaster nodded and took his dinner off to a far table, where he proceeded to prod at it with a fork. (Maybe he ate it, maybe he didn't. This story doesn't give you all the answers. Some things will remain mysterious.)

Cook scooped another ladleful of clown fish and was about to dump it on the next person's plate when he stopped with the long-handled spoon poised in mid-air.

'Oh, it's you,' he said.

'Yes,' said Dr Surprise, unable to fault the chef's deduction. He leant closer, looked at Cook from behind his monocle and said something so quietly that Fizz couldn't hear what it was. Cook shook his head. Dr Surprise said something else. Cook looked angry and shook his head again.

This was the quietest argument Fizz had ever not heard.

The Doctor stood up straight. 'When?' he said.

'Soon,' said Cook, pouring the contents of the ladle onto the Doctor's plate.

'And a carrot, please,' said the Doctor. 'For Flopples.'

Cook reached into his back pocket and pulled out a small orange carrot. He handed it over.

'Thank you.'

At the same time as this very quiet argument, Fizz had observed something else going on. While Cook and the Doctor talked, the slick black shape of Fish, the circus's sea lion, was sneaking through the kitchen, across to the trays of cooked fish, where he immediately began wolfing down as big mouthfuls as he could manage. And this was what he was doing when Cook turned round and saw him.

Uh-oh, Fizz thought.

If there'd been a handle to hand, Cook would've flown off it. Since there wasn't, he threw his ladle at Fish.

The sea lion lifted his head at just that moment. His face was covered with thick white fishy sauce, which his fat black tongue was quickly cleaning off, and he wasn't paying attention to flying utensils. The ladle caught him just above the eye with a loud *bonk!* and went spinning off to clatter into the kitchen.

Cook followed the ladle with some of his choicest swear words, loudly accusing Fish of ruining everyone's dinner by sticking his smelly filthy head in their food. This wasn't the first time this had happened, and frankly, Cook said, he'd had enough. He was fed up with the greedy sea lion gobbling everything he could find. He hardly had time to cook, he added, having to constantly watch out for thieves. He pointed out (also) that a sea lion should be out in the ocean, not cluttering up a man's kitchen, licking pans and sniffing bowls. Fish was a very naughty sea lion indeed, Cook concluded, and on the whole, as the circus chef, he was rather annoyed.

(You'll notice I'm paraphrasing what Cook said, which means saying what he said but in different words. I'm not telling you the actual words for two main reasons. Firstly, if I did, your parents or teachers would take this book off you right now and bring it straight back to the bookshop or library. They might even make a complaint to the publishers too, and *they* get tetchy enough hearing from *me*, let

alone from unhappy bookbuyers. And secondly, even if I *wanted* to use the actual words, I couldn't, because I don't know how to spell most of them. They were *that* rude.)

Fizz felt sorry for his friend. He knew the sea lion had done wrong stealing the fish, but he didn't deserve such a loud and public telling off. And he certainly hadn't needed a ladle bounced off his head. The poor thing.

As Cook's tirade (which is another word for a harangue (which is a sort of dessert he rarely made)) went on, Fish sat there, stunned. He wasn't used to being shouted at. He wasn't used to having things thrown at him, and even less to things hitting him. He was the cheeky sea lion everyone loved, wasn't he?

But Cook clearly didn't think so, and even as the Ringmaster put his hand on the chef's shoulder and told him to calm down, Fish was waddling out of the Mess Tent, a sorry look on his face, his head hung low and his whiskers drooping.

When it came to show time, a little later, Fish was gone. Wystan looked everywhere he could think of, but the sea lion wasn't to be found. He'd left and not come back. And since Wystan couldn't do his act by himself, he had to sit the evening out.

(This is where the flashback ends. The next bit's no longer in the same sort of black and white that this last bit's been in, it's in the *normal* black and white instead. I hope that's clear.)

So, bearing all that in mind, Fizz was surprised to see his friend so excited after the show.

 18

'Listen,' Wystan said, breathlessly (and still between pants). 'I was lying on my bed, combing my beard, when I thought I heard something *outside*. This was when you were all, you know, doing the show. So I looked out the window and there was this bloke creeping around by the cages. Dead dodgy-looking.'

Wystan slept in the spare bedroom of Miss Tremble's caravan. She trained the horses and was a woman of delicate, sensitive feelings. Her caravan was always parked next to the animals, alongside the portable paddock where her horses spent the night stood up sleeping. Charles's cage and Fish's inflatable pool were round there too. (It was only a paddling pool, but every now and the sea lion liked to have a quick splash in the night in between mackerel-ful dreams.)

 19

'He had this pirate's hat on and his chin stuck out like it was reaching for something, like Mr Punch's, and instead of a hand he had . . . a hook.' Wystan let this description hang in the air for moment, before finishing it off with what seemed to be incontrovertible proof of wrongdoing. 'And underneath his nose,' he said, 'he had *no moustache at all.*'

'That's weird,' said Fizz, nodding sagely.

'Yeah, that's what I thought. He was being all creepy round the animals' cages, all tiptoeing and peering over his shoulder . . .' Wystan mimed the look, with one hand curled into a claw and his beard sticking out like a chin (although not very convincingly) '. . . and he was halfway up the steps to Captain Fox-Dingle's caravan when there was this beeping and he stopped. He froze there, just for a second. Then he quickly looked behind him and scarpered. Not really running, you know, but right annoyed at being disturbed.'

'A beeping?' Fizz asked.

'Yeah, like a digital clock or something,' Wystan said. 'I went to the door, to go out and see which way he went. And you'll never believe what happened then.'

'Did he try to sell you a digital watch?'

'No, don't be stupid. I opened the door, and there, straight in front of me, was a flipping crocodile!'

'A crocodile?' asked Fizz, sceptically.

'Yeah, a great big thing, waddling along on the grass between the caravans.'

'A crocodile,' Fizz repeated.

'Yes, a crocodile. Huge mouth, with loads of teeth.'

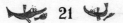

'What did you do?'

'What do you think? I shut the door quick. By the time I got back to the window, it had gone. They'd both gone.'

'If they were there at all.' Fizz thought the story sounded distinctly fishy.

'Of course they were there,' Wystan snapped. 'I was nearly eaten by a crocodile.'

'You weren't nearly eaten though, were you?' said Fizz. 'You *hid* from it.'

'What would you have done, then?'

'I'd've wrestled it to the ground and then called for help,' Fizz said.

There was a short, embarrassing silence. The light bulbs strung between the caravans and the Big Top swung gently in the cold evening breeze, flickering to themselves like dim yellow-orange fruits. Wystan gave Fizz a look from over the top of his beard that said, 'Yeah, right.'

Fizz shuffled his feet and changed the subject. 'So who do you reckon this strange chap was?'

'First I thought,' Wystan said, 'maybe he was a friend of the Captain's?'

Fizz shook his head. 'Then why would he be sneaking round?'

'Exactly, that's why I done away with the idea,' said Wystan.

'Maybe,' Fizz offered, 'he was the new assistant Miss Tremble's been talking about. She said she needed a new groom to help her since Alberto joined the navy. Maybe he was looking for her, and just got the caravans muddled up.'

'Well, he'd be a right rum groom, what with that hook and all. You'd be a brave horse

to be stroked by him. And anyway, she'd've told me if she'd been and hired someone.'

'Well, I don't know who he could be then,' Fizz said, his brain almost empty of ideas.

'I had one idea,' said Wystan. 'One more.'

'What?'

'I reckon he's a *saboteur*, come from another circus.'

'A saboteur?'

'Yeah, come to sabotage the circus. Make us look bad.'

'Twice in one summer?' Fizz asked, referring to what had happened in *Fizzlebert Stump and the Bearded Boy*. (Wystan scuffed his feet in the dust, embarrassed, thinking about his part in that book.) 'Bit unlikely, isn't it?' Fizz racked his brains to think of another explanation. 'He was probably an audience

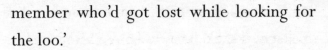

member who'd got lost while looking for the loo.'

Wystan looked at Fizz. He mimed the hook. He mimed the chin (though not very well). He mimed the lack of moustache. He mimed the man's tiptoeing spy-ish-ness. And he mimed the lugubrious waddle of a hungry crocodile.

'Fancy dress?' Fizz offered.

'You're an idiot sometimes,' Wystan harrumphed.

'No I'm not,' Fizz replied.

'Yes you are.'

'No I'm not.'

'Yes you are.'

'No I'm not.'

Wystan stepped right up close, so that his beard tickled our hero's chin. It bristled and crackled with tense static electricity.

'Yes, you are,' he said quietly and menacingly.

'Ah, my happy boys!' said Fizz's mum, looking round the edge of the doorway.

'Hello, Mrs Stump,' Wystan said, stepping back and waving at her with the tip of his beard.

'It's time for bed, darling,' she said, looking at Fizz. 'It's a big day tomorrow.'

'Mum!'

'But darling,' she said, nodding seriously, 'there was a thing on the news about it. The Prime Minister has decided that Thursdays will be twenty-six hours long. Starting tomorrow. A big day.'

'But . . .'

Even as Fizz spoke he was trying to see whether she still had any clown's makeup on.

'Um . . .' Wystan lifted his finger as he spoke, 'ain't tomorrow Monday?'

'It was on the news,' Mrs Stump answered. 'Mondays are the new Thursday.'

'But . . .'

Fizz was pretty sure he could see a bit of white face paint on her left cheek.

'Oh, just go to bed, Wystan,' he said,

knowing when to give up arguing with a clown. 'It's getting late.'

Wystan looked at Mrs Stump again and then at Fizz and whispered, 'What about . . . ?'

'It was nothing,' Fizz said. 'I reckon you fell asleep and just dreamt it all.'

'Well, I ain't dreaming now, am I?' Wystan muttered under his breath. 'And I weren't dreaming then, and you're an idiot to say I was.' And with that he shoved his hands in his pockets, turned on the spot and stomped off between the caravans, leaving Fizz and his mum behind.

Fizz hadn't said what he really thought, which was that Wystan had made the whole story up to make it seem he'd had an exciting evening even though he wasn't performing in the Big Top. And the reason Fizz hadn't actually come out and said this was that he was polite, and his mum's interruption had taken the wind out of the boys' argument.

Nevertheless as Fizz shook his head and climbed the steps into the caravan, he half hoped Wystan had been right (although, of course, Fizz knew he wasn't), because a strange-looking nautical man pursued by a crocodile did sound *vaguely* interesting.

CHAPTER TWO

In which some questions are asked
and in which a lion is discussed

The next morning Fizzlebert woke up, got up and ate up his breakfast. As he swallowed the last slice of doughnut on toast, wiping a spot of red jam from his chin, he began to tell his mum and dad about Wystan's story. (The more he thought about it the sillier it seemed.)

'Guess what Wystan told me,' he began.

'Don't talk with your mouth full, Fizz,' his mum said.

'But I've finished eating. It's not full.'

'I know, dear,' Mrs Stump said, putting salt on her cornflakes, 'but it's good advice. In general.'

Fizz nodded and had another go at telling them about Wystan's stranger. To his amusement, his dad seemed to take it seriously.

'A hook, you say?' he said after Fizz had finished.

'That's what Wystan said.'

'I can't think of anyone with a hook. Gloria, how about you?'

'No,' said Mrs Stump. 'I haven't got a hook.'

She waved her hands in the air. They were small, pink and ended with the usual number of wiggling fingers. She looked surprised that her husband had had to ask. Or maybe she just looked surprised because of the makeup. Fizz wasn't sure.

'No dear,' his dad said. 'I meant, have you seen anyone matching Fizz's description?'

'Oh yes,' she said, brightly.

'Really?'

Both Fizz and his dad looked at her, half intrigued to hear what she'd seen, and half prepared for clown-induced disappointment.

'Where?' asked Mr Stump.

'I saw him last night,' Mrs Stump replied, mysteriously. 'I was just looking out the front door and there was this chap, stood right in front of the caravan. Bold as brass buttons. He was talking with that nice bearded fellow, that Barboozul boy.'

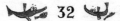

Fizz's stomach flipped. Had Wystan been telling the truth? And had his mum seen Wystan *talking* to the hook-handed stranger? How could that have been? Why? When?

And then he remembered.

'Mum?' he said.

'Yes darling?'

'Are you talking about *me*?'

'Well, it was someone who matched your description, certainly.'

'Oh, Gloria,' Mr Stump said. 'You're just being awkward now. Think properly. Wystan says he saw a stranger. Have you seen a stranger with a hook in the circus? Yes or no?'

'No. Not a one, unless . . . But wait! What about the Ringmaster's brother? Do you remember he visited the circus once, years ago? He had a hook, and . . .'

'No, no,' Mr Stump interrupted, putting his hand to his forehead, 'that wasn't a *hook*. It was a *book*, Gloria. He had a *book*.'

Fizz could see a long and ridiculous conversation beginning, so he slipped down from the table, did up his shoes, opened the caravan door and left them to it.

As Fizz was making his way toward Captain Fox-Dingle's caravan for his first lesson of the day, Wystan wandered over to him.

'Fizz,' he said.

'Wystan,' said Fizz.

'Have you seen Fish this morning?' Wystan asked, rubbing the tip of his beard between two fingers.

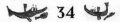 34

'No,' Fizz said. 'Hasn't he come back?'

'I've not seen him,' Wystan answered, 'and neither's anyone I've asked.'

Fizz didn't say anything. He knew how Wystan must be feeling. If Fish didn't turn up then he wouldn't have an act to do for a second night in a row. On top of that, Fizz felt a tingle of worry in his stomach for his missing friend. Just a tingle, because Fish hadn't been gone that long, and he was a grown sea lion, quite capable of looking after himself. Sort of. Unless he got distracted by an open can of tuna.

'There's footprints in the mud,' Wystan said suddenly, changing the subject. 'Exactly where I saw the bloke. So I definitely weren't dreaming.'

'Footprints?' asked Fizz.

'Yeah. *Boot* prints. And not just boot prints, but claw-prints too. Definitely a crocodile.'

'I'll believe them when I see them,' Fizz said.

'Well, come on,' Wystan muttered. 'Quick, before some other idiot steps all over them.'

'I suppose,' Fizz said, squinting at the mud, 'that it *could* be a crocodile.'

The boot prints were just boot prints, and in a circus there are a lot of people wearing boots every day. But the claw prints did look like claws, although there were only a few of them, the rest presumably having been over-printed by the many boots of the circus.

Fizz had read a lot of books and seen lots of pictures, and he was trying to remember exactly what a crocodile's feet looked like when Wystan spoke.

'I had a thought,' he said in a low secretive voice. 'When I found Fish hadn't come back this morning. When no one had seen him anywhere, I put two and two together.'

'Did you get four?' Fizz asked, looking up from the mud.

'No,' Wystan replied. 'I got "a hook-handed pirate bloke and his pet crocodile have kidnapped our sea lion".'

'I think you're supposed to get four,' Fizz said. He wasn't brilliant at maths but this sounded right.

'Don't be stupid,' Wystan said. 'This is the only thing that makes sense.'

'What, that Fish has been kidnapped by a pirate?'

'Yes.'

Fizz didn't know whether to laugh or to be serious. 'So, what do we do now?' he said, adopting the serious tone on the outside.

'I dunno,' Wystan said. 'I guess we rescue him.'

'And how do we do that?' Fizz asked. 'The prints don't help us. That's your only clue.'

'Yeah,' said Wystan rubbing his beard between his fingers. 'That ain't no good. I guess we just gotta keep our eyes open. You know, for *other* clues.'

'Right,' Fizz said, sounding just like he agreed. 'And in the meantime, we'd better go to art class.'

When they knocked on Captain Fox-Dingle's caravan door he instantly didn't answer it.

Instead he called to them from Charles's cage, which was to one side of the caravan.

'Here,' he snapped in his usual clipped manner.

Captain Fox-Dingle was a man of few words, only a tiny number of which were verbs. It was rumoured that he'd been in the army once, and communicating quickly is an important skill for soldiers. In the heat of the heart of battle there's no time for faffing about with long sentences full of conjunctions, and sub-clauses, such as this one, and brackets (like these): no, it's all about keeping it brief – 'Run!' 'Fight!' 'Duck!' 'Ouch!' 'Cake!', and so on. In civilian life, once he'd joined the circus as their lion tamer, he'd maintained this shorthand manner, and over the years Fizz had learnt to fill in the gaps in his head.

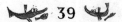

As well as lion taming, the Captain also took Fizz and Wystan for lessons. In the circus all the boys' lessons were taught by different acts (Dr Surprise took them for history, Madame Plume de Matant for French and so on) and it just so happened Captain Fox-Dingle had drawn the short straw, and had drawn it so well, the Ringmaster had made him their art teacher.

The boys walked over to the cage.

The Captain was sat on a stool inside it. His uniform glittered in the sunlight. It was ornate and had gold piping round the edges and across the pockets. His hat had a peak that shaded his eyes, and a logo, a coat of arms, on the front: a fox and a lion facing each other across a chair, enclosed in a circle which, if you looked closely, was made from a whip. The Captain had drawn the design himself.

He had small dark eyes that were always watching out for *something* and a flat nose, as if he'd been in some fights when he was younger but hadn't always won them. Underneath the nose was a neat little toothbrush of a moustache. He stood up as stiff as he spoke and if you didn't know him you'd be forgiven for thinking he was a villain. (If it weren't for the fact that his uniform was bright pink.)

'What's wrong with the lion?' Wystan said, pointing at Charles, who was lying in the corner by the Captain's stool.

'Old.'

'Oh, Charles,' Fizz said, kneeling beside the cage and looking at the cat.

Charles was resting his big chin on his front paws and had his eyes closed. His magnificent mane looked droopier than normal. As Fizz patted his nose the lion gave a big heave of a sigh, and a little whine of a wheeze whistled with it through the bars of the cage.

'Oh, you poor thing,' Fizz said.

'Fizz,' said Captain Fox-Dingle. 'No show.'

Fizz absorbed these words and made them into a sentence.

'You don't think he'll be up for the show tonight?'

Captain Fox-Dingle shook his head.

'Is he sick?' Wystan asked. 'Has he caught flu or something?'

Fizz looked at Wystan. When he'd thought it was just the bearded boy who didn't have a show to do, he'd been unhappy for him, but not worried like he was feeling now. To think *he* didn't have an act to do either – that was dreadful. No circus performer ever liked missing out, being told they couldn't do their act. They weren't in showbiz in order to sit in the wings all night. Who was?

'Not flu,' said Captain Fox-Dingle. 'Old.'

'How old *is* Charles, Captain?' asked Fizz.

Captain Fox-Dingle looked at his fingers and counted.

'Very,' he said eventually. He laid a hand on

the top of Charles's head and ruffled his great shaggy mane.

'But the act went so well last night,' Fizz protested. 'It was perfect.'

'Good show.'

Captain Fox-Dingle shrugged and sat silently for a minute. The sadness of the moment seeped into them all.

'What's he going to do if he can't do his act?' Wystan asked.

'Retirement. Good home.'

At least, Fizz thought, trying to put a brave face on things, Charles could enjoy his last years somewhere nice. He knew the Captain would find a good home for him, because the Captain cared deeply about his friend. But Fizz had known Charles all his life. How strange the circus would be without him.

'So last night was his last show?' he asked.

'Maybe.'

'Perhaps he'll perk up tomorrow?'

'Maybe.'

As he said this word Captain Fox-Dingle's bottom lip quivered, in exactly the way it would were he upset. His tiny smart moustache bristled as he sighed. His eyes were fixed just to left of the boys, gripping the distance tightly in their gaze.

There was no art class that morning. The boys could tell the Captain wasn't in the mood and they didn't mind skipping a lesson or two.

If they skipped a lesson, however, then they'd have to find something else to do. And to find out what that 'something else' is, I'll have to get on and write the next chapter.

CHAPTER THREE

In which Dr Surprise surprises
the boys and in which an Aquarium
is visited

After half an hour of staring closely at the ground in different places round the circus, between caravans and tents, around cages and trucks, the two boys had found almost no further traces of the crocodile. (*Almost* no traces because they did see one print that looked a bit like a clawed reptilian foot, but it was at the bottom of the steps to

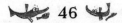

Luke Longrope's caravan, and everyone knew he wore crocodile-skin cowboy boots.)

They were despondent. They scuffed their feet and hung their heads. This wasn't helping them find Fish, or find the kidnappers. They were rubbish detectives. The *most* rubbish, Fizz thought. Dreadful detectives. Their sea lion friend was out there somewhere and they'd probably never see him again and it was all their fault. Oh, woe was them.

Thankfully, their moping was interrupted at that point. (If I was a better author I'd've interrupted it earlier, but never mind, eh?)

'Ah, Fizzlebert,' said Dr Surprise. 'I thought I might find you here.'

It was no surprise that Dr Surprise had known where to find him. After all, the mind reader was a mind reader, and also he'd seen them walking past his caravan window less than three minutes earlier.

'The Captain,' the Doctor went on, 'told me about Charles. It's a sad thing, Fizz.'

It was a sad thing, Fizz agreed. Showlessness. Both boys were out of an act tonight, unless they could find Fish, and that wasn't looking likely (see above). He felt like a spare wheel. The only time a spare wheel is needed is when you've got a puncture, but unfortunately, with both him and Wystan out of the show, it was like being a spare wheel *with* a puncture. They'd both be sitting backstage tonight, watching the show through the curtains, passing Percy Late his plate and keeping Flopples's after-show carrot warm for the Doctor.

'I thought you might appreciate a change

of scenery, boys. Take your minds off things. How do you fancy visiting the Aquarium?'

'Aquarium?' Fizz asked.

'A big building full of fish,' explained Dr Surprise.

'I know that,' Fizz replied. 'I just meant "What Aquarium?"'

'Oh, whichever one's nearest,' said Dr Surprise, reaching into his pocket for his pocket watch and glancing as if to check the time. At this point he noticed that his hand was empty.

'Where's your watch, Doctor?' asked Wystan.

'I keep forgetting,' Dr Surprise replied, 'it's at the watch-mender's in town, being mended. Flopples mistook it for a carrot last weekend, and, well . . .'

Fizz had been wondering why the Doctor's act these last few days had involved lots of sparks, mind-reading and magic tricks, but none of his famous hypnotism. This explained it, since he always dangled his pocket watch when he put people into trances. Without it he was just a normal man with a top hat, monocle, dangerous rabbit, card tricks, unexpected fireworks and surprising bunches of flowers.

'There's an Aquarium I spotted just along the prom,' Dr Surprise went on, putting the non-existent pocket watch back into his existent waistcoat pocket. 'Won't take us five minutes to walk there. It *could* be interesting. I've heard that they have a lesser green-footed coral octopus in there that can disguise itself so well that it completely vanishes. It changes colour and shape and the texture of its skin and all sorts, and, hey presto!, you simply can't see it any more. Sounds like marvellous stuff. Or so someone said. I wouldn't know anything about it.'

'Yeah, okay,' the boys said. 'Why not?'

This would be a good time to tell you where the circus is. As you know, Fizz's home is a travelling circus and this means every week or so they move from one place to another, parking up in a town park and setting up the Big Top to entertain the locals. So, where's the circus today?

It's by the seaside.

If you look into the sky you'll see gulls circling. If you look closer you'll see the gulls are seagulls. And they're still circling.

The circus is set up in a park, one side of which faces the sea. There's a row of trees, then the tarmac strip of a path and then a rather pebbly beach and then water. Lots of water, water as far as you can see. In the other direction the park opens out into the town, which is just like any other town, except with more fish and chip shops, seashell emporia and concrete sandcastles. (Since the beaches in these parts are singly shingly, a bright-eyed Mayor in the 1980s had half a dozen giant sandcastles built out of concrete around the town (in the parks, squares, shopping centres and so on). He claimed they reflected the cheery seaside nature of the town, without the impermanence, the mutability if you will, of a normal sandcastle (that is to say, the sea can't sweep them away, because they're great ugly things made out of concrete). He said they'd bring in tourists. Tourists disagreed.)

A more recent Mayor (the current one in fact) preferred to attract tourists with big posters advertising his '*Summer Season Festival of Fun!!!*' The circus had been booked as the main entertainment and had been parked in the park for just over a week. They had one more night here before the festival ended and the tents got packed away and they trundled off to a new town.

Fizz had been busy with circus work and his lessons, and had hardly had time to stroll on the beach, let alone go exploring along the prom. But now he had nothing but time on his hands. A little exploring wouldn't go amiss.

* * *

They walked along the path that led out of the park, the sea on one side and the town on the other. At the seaside any path or pavement that stretches between beach and buildings isn't called a path or pavement. It's a 'prom', or 'promenade' for long. The Victorians liked to walk up and down looking at the sea on one side and the urchins on the other (although sea urchins would be on the sea side, of course), and that's (sort of) what 'promenade' means in French, which isn't what the Victorians spoke (except the French ones), but is what they called it anyway. (That explanation got a little more complicated than I expected, but is still shorter and clearer than the explanation Dr Surprise gave Fizz and Wystan as they walked, and which happened while I just did all this describing and explaining. So be thankful for small mercies.)

A hundred yards out of the park, the scene
on the left changed from a grey shingle beach
to a grey shingle beach with an old fishing
boat hauled up on it. There were seagulls sat
in a row on its bulwarks (which is another
way of saying they were sat on its gunnels,
which are the bits of a ship's side that stick up
like a tiny wall around the deck's edge). They
squawked and cawed as the little party went

by. (Not 'party' like a birthday party, of course, just 'party' like a small group made up of a mind reader and his two short friends, which would be a very disappointing birthday party, unless you only have one friend and enjoy mind readers, in which case it's pretty much perfect.)

Ignoring my descriptive writing, Fizz and his friends continued towards the Aquarium, which they could see sat square at the other end of the prom. It was a large white-washed building, thick and squat and irregularly-shaped, like a jumble of building blocks. Its doors were wide open and over them large friendly letters spelt out the word 'QUARIUM', which would have looked better if the first 'A' of the word hadn't fallen off when a particularly fat seagull had landed on it.

Fizz had never been in an aquarium before and he wondered what it would be like. The only fish he knew anything about were the sort that lay on plates, unmoving and dribbling vinegar. The sort that went well with potatoes (another thing he'd never seen in their natural environment, or even in a potatoarium (or greengrocers, as they're more usually known)). What would fish be like alive and in action?

Well, only time would tell.

It took a minute to walk to the doors. It took less than a minute for Dr Surprise to buy three tickets, and then two minutes to untangle Wystan, who'd got his beard caught in the turnstile.

Then they were in.

And all around Fizz, filling every wall,

were tank after tank of water, filled with a hundred different examples of very dull fish.

Looking into one tank he could see big grey fish that swam to the right, turned around and swam back to the left, and in another there were small grey fish that did the same, only the other way round. There were pebbles that sat at the bottom of the tanks looking only slightly less action-packed than the fish. One tank had a miniature statue of an old-fashioned diver leaning at a jaunty angle in it, but even that wasn't enough to keep Fizz's attention.

Though the fish were incredibly dull, he couldn't help but think of what Fish might've thought of the place. The silly sea lion would've loved it. Of course, it would have been dangerous to let him loose in there. Fizz

could imagine the broken glass and the spilling water and the guzzled fish . . .

It would at least have been more interesting than this.

He sighed loudly. Wystan joined in.

'Well, I expect the *really* exciting stuff is further on,' said Dr Surprise, peering into an empty tank that almost certainly didn't contain an octopus in disguise. (It contained a lot of air and a sign on the front saying UNDER RENOVATION, and a sign under that saying UNDER 'UNDER RENOVATION'.)

Next to it was another empty tank.

'That's odd,' Wystan said, pointing at it.

Although it was filled with water and there were weeds in it moving slowly in the current from a little pump, there were no fish in there, just a sign pasted on the glass, which read: THESE FISH HAVE BEEN STOLEN. BY THIEVES. WE APOLOGISE FOR THE DISAPPOINTMENT. Then there was a phone number for anyone with any information about the theft to ring.

'Who'd steal a fish?' Fizz asked.

'Well, Fish would,' Wystan said.

'Yeah, but he can't work door handles and he wouldn't have stopped at just the one fish, would he?'

They turned around to show the sign to the Doctor, but he'd already wandered off. There was only one way he could've gone, so the boys trotted along after him.

Turning a corner Fizz saw Dr Surprise peering into tanks in a corridor filled with blue fish. Through the doorway at the end he caught a glimpse of a room that flashed with yellow light, which he reckoned was a yellow fish room. So, the aquarium was colour-coded. Fizz had worried it was just going to be grey fish all the way through.

The blue fish were slightly more interesting than the grey ones. A few of them had weird huge mouths with spindly teeth, some had fins frail as lace doilies, and some were such a bright blue it hurt your eyes to look at, which made Wystan and Fizz look at them even more.

They stumbled past a couple more tanks with 'Stolen Fish' signs on them and wobbled dizzily into the yellow room, and from there followed the Doctor into a room of green fish.

'Oh!' said Dr Surprise.

'What is it?' asked Fizz, wondering if something interesting had happened.

The Doctor was staring intently into an empty tank. Like the other tanks it was filled with water and a few gently waving fronds of seaweed. But apart from that, as far as Fizz could see, it was devoid of contents. Oddly, it had no sticker stuck on the glass.

'It's just another empty tank,' Wystan said, tapping the glass with his knuckle.

'Ah, Mr Barboozul,' Dr Surprise said, 'there you are wrong. *This* is the wonderful lesser green-footed coral octopus. Look at the way she hides. Absolutely beautiful. So clever. So perfect! So exquisite! How much I admire her talents.'

The boys squinted and peered and looked really hard, but saw nothing.

'There's nothing in there, Doctor,' Fizz said. 'You're pulling our legs.'

'This is a fine octopus, Fizzlebert, and you're very lucky to have seen it.'

'You mean "to have *not* seen it",' Wystan grumbled as he turned away from the glass.

(There's a theory that says every zoo has at least one cage or area filled with trees and bushes and *no animals*, and that next to this area they all have a sign with the name of a really interesting animal on; say, a tiger. Crowds of people spend hours looking into the empty cage saying things like, 'Oh, I think he's up the back there,' and 'Do you see, just in that shadow, under the big tree?' or 'They must be off sleeping somewhere.' And even though no one sees the tiger they're never annoyed by the empty cage with the interesting label, because humans have a deeply held belief that wild animals *should* be hard to spot, and so the empty cage experience in some way feels more *worthwhile* than the enclosure where the polar bear lies in full sight, in the open, sulking on a concrete beach next to a pond of stagnant water.

In fact, there's a second theory that says a zoo *could* be constructed entirely of empty enclosures, empty cages and interesting labels, and that this would be a deeply satisfying experience for the visitors, who would enjoy the challenge of spotting the rare and elusive animals, and much more fun for the animals, who wouldn't have to live in cages any more.

As far as I know, such a zoo hasn't yet been built, or if it has, no one has noticed.)

'No, I still can't see anything,' Fizz said, turning away.

And then he saw something.

BRAND NEW, the poster behind him announced, SEA-LIFE SPECTACULAR, DEATH-DEFYING STUNTS THREE TIMES DAILY – 11AM, 1PM, 3PM.

Whenever the words 'death-defying' appear, the ears of a circus performer perk up, and Fizz's ears did just that (which was

weird, since he'd read the sign with his eyes).
Death-defying stunts had to be better than
deathly-dull fish and non-existent octopuses.

He looked at his watch.

It was almost eleven now, so he dragged
Wystan and the Doctor from in front of the
empty tank.

They pushed through a set of swing doors
and found themselves outside, in front of an
enormous pool. Water lapped with a calm
gurgle across the tiled poolside and the
sudden gust of fresh air smelt briskly sea-y.
Gulls circled noisily overhead and the high
stands of seats were filled with as many as
several people.

On the opposite side of the pool was a
concrete stage, backed by a wall with a
curtained doorway in it. The wall ran from the

side of the main Aquarium building, but only for a few metres. Beyond that the stage area dwindled away into the pool, which lapped against a low wall, beyond which was the sea. Or at least the sight of the sea: they were probably higher up than high tide could reach them here, but Fizz could see a sailing boat out in the distance and bobbing white specks which were more gulls. It was quite a view.

Our circus trio shuffled along the front row of the seating, apologised their way past a woman who was sat with a notebook and pen on her lap ('Press,' Dr Surprise said to himself, meaning she was from a newspaper, not that anyone should touch anything), and sat down right in the middle.

There was a drum roll, and then tinny recorded music echoed round the watery

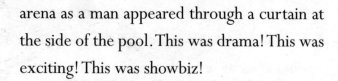

arena as a man appeared through a curtain at the side of the pool. This was drama! This was exciting! This was showbiz!

On his head was a nineteenth-century sea captain's hat, on his body was a long heavy navy blue coat with brass buttons, on his top lip was no moustache at all and in his hand he held a silvery fish.

No!

Fizz looked again, just as Wystan began nudging him. He *didn't* hold a silvery fish in his hand. He had a silvery fish *stuck*, *impaled*, *pierced* if you will, on the end of a curving metal hook, exactly where his hand would have been, had it not been replaced with a hook. And a fish.

'Told you so,' muttered Wystan, and Fizz had to admit that he had.

CHAPTER FOUR

In which some flying fish fly and in
which a sea lion is seen

'**L**adies and gentlemen, boys and girls,'
the nautical gentleman began, his
voice amplified and echoing round as the
music died away to a background murmur. 'I
am Admiral Spratt-Haddock and this is my
world famous *'Quarium Spectacular*. Today you
will see things you never dreamt of, things
unparalleled in their excitement, unrivalled

in their oddity, unequalled in their sheer fishiness. Just wait! Witness daring displays of synchronised squirting squid! Fantastic flapping free-flying flying fish! And more, much more. And after all that, there's . . . oh, but wait, what's this?'

The music perked up, a jaunty little funny tune, as, from behind the curtain, a sleek low brown shape ran, leapt in the air, snatched the fish from Admiral Spratt-Haddock's hook where it had been dangling by his side, and dove headfirst into the water. It all happened so fast Fizz didn't know what it had been until Dr Surprise whispered, 'I *think* that was an otter.'

'Oh, Philip!' the hook-handed host said, his bright voice echoing round the arena as he laughed. 'That wasn't *your* fish, that was *my* lunch.' He turned around and hooked another fish out of the metal bucket that sat beside the back wall. 'Now, where have you got to?'

The Admiral leant out and peered into the water, trying to see where the otter had gone. He didn't notice Philip slide out of the pool. The otter tiptoed behind him, keeping his eyes on the Admiral's back, before slowly lifting a fish from the bucket with its teeth. It looked sideways at the other fish hanging on the hook, then looked at where Fizz was sat, and he could have sworn the otter winked at him. Then, in a flash Philip snatched the Admiral's dangling hooked fish and did a somersault backwards into the water. Once safely out in the middle of the pool the otter clambered up onto a large log that was floating smack in the middle of the pool and began to eat his prize.

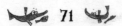

'Philip!'

Fizz laughed at this, and heard his laughter echoing round the empty arena. His performer's heart wished that there had been a crowd there to appreciate the comedy of the act. He looked around, and saw that Wystan was frowning at him.

'That's *him*,' the bearded boy hissed, pointing at the figure on the stage, 'how can you laugh?' Fizz realised that the unlikely funny otteriness of the show had momentarily outweighed his suspicion of this 'Admiral'.

But just because he'd been sneaking round the circus, that didn't mean he was a bad guy, did it? After all, there might've been a perfectly innocent explanation, Fizz thought, especially now it turned out he was in show business too. Maybe he was looking for Captain Fox-Dingle to discuss animal training things. Maybe Fish really had just wandered off.

All the same, he had to admit, this Admiral did *look* suspicious.

The show moved on. A shoal of flying fish soared above the water, flying in intricate patterns over the otter who still lay calmly on his log, floating in the middle of the pool. Their wing-fins glittered like rainbows in the midday sunlight, rustling like the pages of riffling library books. They looked like dragonflies, he thought, but damp fishy ones. The display was as beautiful as Philip's act had been funny.

'At this point,' the Admiral said, rubbing his ear with that glinting hook, 'normally you'd be witness to the astonishing music of Craddock the Choral Cod, but, just last night he was . . . he was . . . stolen. This morning, land-lubbers, I opened the 'Quarium doors, and his tank was empty. Craddock's gone, and his beautiful song gone with him.'

The Admiral looked angry and upset. Of course, Fizz knew what it was like to lose someone. He and Wystan were both missing Fish. At that thought he smiled slightly. The Admiral was missing fish too. The only difference was a capital letter.

Admiral Spratt-Haddock stood silent, staring out at the ranks of seats, most of which were empty. Fizz wondered if he was going to say something else, or whether the show was over already.

But it wasn't. A shoal of synchronised goldfish swam under the water in the shapes of popular celebrities; a school of eels did simple sums (not terribly well, but still, they were eels); and a squadron of squid squirted water at different-sized tin cans lined up along the lip of the pool.

Finally Admiral Spratt-Haddock hushed the imaginary noise down (Fizz could imagine the noise a real crowd would have been making quietening), the music diminished to a murmur and he looked around.

'Now me lovely landlubbers,' he said, as if he were imparting a secret, 'we reach the finale, the grand spectacle. This morning you will see here at the 'Quarium, a *brand new* act. Would you please put your hands together and hold your breaths for the astonishing, the amazing, the absolutely unique Pescado, the Sea Lion of Dreams!'

There was a drum roll and then . . .

. . . nothing happened.

Fizz wondered if this was yet another act that had gone missing.

Admiral Spratt-Haddock said his cue again, 'The absolutely unique Pes—'

A head poked through the curtain and honked.

Fizz recognised those whiskers. He recognised that nose. He recognised that honk.

The head looked around, big black eyes mournful and cute like a limping puppy abandoned on the steps of an orphanage on Christmas Eve.

'Oh, *there* you are, you rascal,' said the Admiral, waving a fish on the end of his hook.

The sea lion waddled out from the curtain, nose up, eyes wide, following the scent of the dangling pilchard. He wore a spangly sequined waistcoat and honked excitedly.

'Fish!' Fizz shouted.

He stood up in his seat. Wystan was standing beside him.

'Fish?' Dr Surprise said.

'Look at the waistcoat!' Fizz said.

'Look at the whiskers!' Wystan added.

On the little poolside stage the sea lion had gobbled the fish and rolled over, gulped down another fish and done a handstand, and

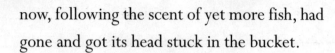

now, following the scent of yet more fish, had gone and got its head stuck in the bucket.

'Oh dear,' said the Admiral, in such a tone of voice as to make an audience aware that this was still part of the act.

With the bucket on his head the sea lion was clattering about by the side of the stage. He banged into the wall and then stepped to the left. His flipper flapped on the first step of a flight of concrete stairs which led up and up to a platform thirty feet above the pool.

'Pescado,' the Admiral said like a bad actor, half-winking at the audience, 'not that way. Don't go up there.'

But the sea lion was determined and, flipper by flipper, he pulled himself up the steps, galvanised bucket rattling, echoing metallic honks punctuating the climb.

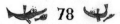

There was nothing the boys could do. Fizz wanted to run out and pull Fish's tail, take the bucket off, save him from those stairs, but a large plastic screen blocked the pool from his reach (it had stopped them all from getting wet when the squids had amusingly misfired their squirts). Dr Surprise quietly suggested they sit down.

'But it's Fish!' Fizz said to him.

'Nonsense,' the Doctor replied. 'Do sit down, boys.'

As they argued, the sea lion reached the top platform and, in a movement so simple as to prove it had all been an act, tossed the bucket into the air, balanced it on his nose, flapped his flippers in a damp clap and honked a triumphant honk that echoed for seconds round and about.

Then in a swift startling move he flicked the bucket into the air, wriggled off the platform and plunged like a beautiful spinning brick nose-first into the water. So deft was the dive that hardly a ripple arose, hardly a splash sploshed, but a startled flurry of flying fish fanned out in a circle, leaping up into the air from the middle of the pool, fleeing like pigeons from a snapping dog.

It was a spectacular dive and only after everything had settled down did Fizz realise he'd been holding his breath.

With a splash the bucket landed in the water, upside down but floating. From underneath the sea lion nudged the bucket round, and rose up in the water balancing it on his nose, honking again. Only then did Fizz notice

Philip the otter in the bucket, looking round in the air as if in surprise.

As he watched open-mouthed at this finale, the showman in him overriding his suspicions, he heard a beeping.

Beep beep beep. Beep beep beep.

It sounded like an electric alarm clock at the beginning of another long day.

As the audience looked around to see where the odd sound had come from Fizz noticed Admiral Spratt-Haddock drop his head into his hands, and then a roar of water splashed up out of the centre of the pool.

The log that Philip the otter had been so calmly lying on throughout the show had reared up, split apart, and lunged at the sea lion with his balanced bucket.

And Fizz saw, with a start, that it wasn't a log after all, it was a crocodile, and it was chasing the sea lion out of the pool. A loud snap of its jaws and a flick of its long tail saw stillness return to the arena. Once again it looked like a large green-brown log was drifting in the middle of the water, and the Admiral and his prize sea lion (who was also Fizz and Wystan's prize sea lion) were stood on the concrete beside the pool looking out at the rippling water.

Spratt-Haddock leant down and said something into Fish's ear the boys couldn't make out, but Fizz got the feeling it was an apology.

And then the show was over.

The Admiral, the sea lion and Philip the otter stood in front of the little curtain and

took a bow, and then they all left, and the only sound was the gentle slurp and splash of water on the poolside tiles.

'That *was* Fish,' Fizz said confidently.

'Definitely,' said Wystan. 'I'd know his nose anywhere.'

'That was his waistcoat.'

'Boys,' said the Doctor. 'There is more than one sparkly waistcoat in the world.'

'Not *sparkly*,' corrected Fizz. '*Spangly*.'

The Doctor slapped his knees as if it were some sort of answer. 'I think,' he warbled, raising a finger in the air, 'it's time to go back to the circus. We've been away long enough. A good afternoon's work will take your minds off things.'

With the two grumbling boys in tow the Doctor led his way back through the Aquarium and to the park where the gaily coloured Big Top welcomed them all back home.

Despite what the Doctor said, Fizz and Wystan were decided. They knew their sea lion friend better than anyone. If they couldn't recognise him then who would? He was missing and that Admiral character had been lurking round the circus with his pet crocodile. Everything made perfect sense. His fish had been stolen and so he'd had to steal a Fish of his own.

As they sat with the Doctor in his caravan, they tried to convince him one last time.

'But Fish hasn't been stolen,' Dr Surprise said, stroking Flopples, his white rabbit, who lay in his arms gently snoring. 'He's just wandered off somewhere. He'll be back. He's probably back already. Before you start accusing people,' he went on, 'you must be sure of all the facts. You know that, Fizz. You have to trust me, I looked closely at the Aquarium and that sea lion *wasn't* Fish. I've known him for years, ever since he first arrived at the circus, long before either of you got here. He was a young sea lion then, of course, sneaking fish from behind Cook's back. Oh, it was a big mystery at the time. No one knew where all these fish were going, you see. And Cook was getting angrier and angrier.'

'Like last night?'

'Yes, but this was a different Cook. It was after he left that the chap you know as Cook took over. Before our Cook was Cook, he was just Terry Trapp the escapologist's son. Terry's shuffled off to the great old circus in the sky now, but it's good to have a Trapp still in the circus, as it were.'

'Dr Surprise, what about Fish?'

'Oh, yes, these fish kept going missing. It went on for days. At first Cook blamed the clowns and he banned them from the Mess Tent. They were angry about that, and there are few things worse than angry clowns. They filled his caravan with custard. Got on the roof and poured it through the air vents until it was full. He had to eat his way out. It was definitely not funny at all. But the fish still kept vanishing. *Then* he blamed young Miss Tremble. He thought he'd overheard her ask Unnecessary Sid to get her "some kippers for breakfast". Oh, you should have seen the tears when he accused her. She was mortified. That night the clowns filled Cook's caravan with

horse manure. His tastebuds were never the same after that. The funny thing was it turned out she'd actually asked Unnecessary Sid to buy her some *slippers* in *Belfast*, because he was about to go on holiday you see. To Belfast. And then—'

'Dr Surprise,' Fizz said quietly, adding a cough and lifting his hand as if he were a schoolboy asking a question (which in a way he was).

'Yes?' said Dr Surprise.

'We don't *care* about all that stuff. We only care about Fish *today*,' Wystan snapped. 'We need to rescue him!'

'Rescue him?'

'Yeah, from the Aquarium. Remember?'

'He's been kidnapped, Doctor,' prompted Fizz, in a more friendly tone than Wystan.

(Fizz knew it wasn't a good idea to shout at Dr Surprise. Not only was he sensitive, but Flopples was very protective. Fizz had lost his temper with the Doctor once, when he was much smaller, and he still heard the rabbit's fearsome growl in his nightmares. He didn't want a repeat of that experience.)

'What nonsense, boys,' the Doctor said. 'There's a very special way Fish's whiskers wrinkle when he sniffs. No other sea lion does it quite the same. The Aquarium's Pescado was *not* Fish. Not even close.'

'But it's obvious what's happened,' Wystan said when the boys had left the Doctor's caravan. 'When Cook threw a ladle at Fish last night and shouted at him and ran him out of the Mess Tent, then he must've been so upset that Admiral Spratt-Haddock could easily come along and lure him away.'

'You're right,' Fizz said. 'He looked so upset about being shouted at. All the Admiral had to do was wave a bit of mackerel and smile nicely and he would've followed him anywhere.'

'How did he know, though?' Wystan wondered. 'I mean that Fish was feeling miserable?'

'Well, maybe he just got lucky, maybe he was over here looking for something else, but ran into Fish, or maybe . . . maybe Cook's in cahoots with him?'

'Blimey,' said Wystan, running his fingers through his beard, which was a sign that he was thinking. 'I hadn't thought of that. Cook would love to get rid of Fish, wouldn't he? So

he upset him on purpose, with the Admiral ready and waiting to be nice to him . . .'

'It was all a plot,' Fizz concluded, and Wystan agreed.

And so the boys had dug their way down to the truth of the matter, unearthed the villains, found their friend and worked out the 'why' of the crime. Now all they needed to do was bring the dastardly deed to light, rescue their sea lion and set everything to rights.

Easy.

In fact they'll probably do it all in the next chapter. I expect.

CHAPTER FIVE

In which a plan is set in action and in
which an Aquarium is visited, again

I don't know you. We've not met. I don't
know if you're a boy or a girl, a man or a
woman, a sea lion or a shellfish. I can't possibly know what your life's like, can I? You
might spend lazy sun-filled days on a deck-
chair sitting on the beach sipping fresh mango
juice, humming light-hearted tunes you heard
once in a dream, or you might have people

looking over your shoulder and breathing down your neck, saying, 'Do this. Do that. No, not like this. Do it like that. No, not like that. Over here, not there.'

The life of a boy in a circus isn't a bad life, but it has few deckchairs in it. It is one where people expect you to *do things* and to *be places* at certain times and they get upset if you just go off missing in the middle of the day (unless you're accompanied by a Doctor). So Fizz had to sit through a whole French lesson with Madame Plume de Matant and then his dad lifted him up (with one hand, naturally) so he could clean the windows of their caravan and then he had to sit in the Mess Tent and eat his tea (cod and chips and crispy seaweed, which was a little annoying, since Tuesdays were normally Fizz's favourite, caravan pie (which

is like cottage pie, but moves about more), but while they were at the seaside it was fish every day).

While he was eating he saw Captain Fox-Dingle across the tent. He was just as smart as normal, but the pink of his uniform looked a little dimmer. He was moving his dinner round his plate with his fork but without picking any of it up. It looked like Charles hadn't improved during the day. This wasn't the way a happy lion-tamer went about eating his dinner.

Fizz definitely wouldn't be called upon to do the act tonight.

On any other day he would've been heart-broken to miss out, but his head was still buzzing with Fish and the plan he'd come up with. The job before him, the one he had to do, was to find his friend and free him and return to the circus a hero, wreathed in glory and crowned with triumph.

At the end of it, at least Wystan would have an act again. Maybe he'd let Fizz join in: *Two Boys & A Sea Lion*. It still wouldn't be quite the same as sticking his head in a lion's mouth, though. Nothing could thrill a crowd quite like that.

He'd only done the act the night before, less than twenty-four hours ago, but already he missed Charles and his warm meaty breath. He missed the softness of his fur, and the applause.

He pushed the magnificent land lion out of his mind and filled it up with everything he knew about the sea lion and the Aquarium. *Okay*, he thought, *time to get on with this rescue.*

* * *

He met Wystan outside Miss Tremble's caravan. She'd gone off to give her pre-show pep
talk to her horses and the boys could talk
without being overheard.

'Got everything?' Fizz whispered.

'Why are you whispering, Fizz?' asked
Wystan. 'Tremble's gone to talk to the horses.
there's no one here.'

'Sorry,' said Fizz. 'It's just that going on a

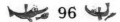

secret rescue mission like this, well, it seems right to whisper.'

Wystan gave him a look over the top of his beard.

'Have you got everything?' Fizz asked again, not loudly, but not so quiet as to be accused of whispering.

Wystan held up a rucksack. 'I got torches, some rope, Fish's spare waistcoat and three tins of tuna.'

'Brilliant. Let's go.'

It was almost seven o'clock. Everyone was busily bustling round, preparing themselves or tending to the crowds, and no one noticed two small shapes sneaking off into the half-dark of the dusk, through the line of trees and out onto the prom.

'That was easy,' Wystan said.

'Well, it *was* the easy part,' Fizz replied.

It was true. Walking away from a busy circus is simple, straightforward, plain sailing. Breaking into a locked Aquarium and finding and freeing and rescuing a sea lion and escaping without getting caught by a dangerous and quite probably mad hook-handed Admiral was going to be a tiny bit harder.

But still, Fizz thought, it *is* going well so far.

They walked along the prom between the park and the Aquarium, past the shingle beach with its one old beached up-tilted fishing boat. They didn't feel the need to tiptoe or to sneak. There was nothing odd-looking about two boys out for an early evening stroll. Nothing at all. They were just doing the perfectly normal sort of thing any perfectly normal sort of person might do.

 98

Except for the beard and the long red ex-Ringmaster's coat, perhaps.

But since there was no one else about (they were probably all at the circus, judging from the crowds the boys had seen queuing before they left) they weren't noticed.

The plan continued to go well, even if 'walking along the prom' was another one of the parts Fizz identified as being easy.

They listened to the crashing waves as they walked along. It sounded like the sea was getting closer and closer. The shingle roared as it was sucked back down the beach with each retreating wave. It sounded, to Fizz's ears, like Charles when he was having his first roar of the morning. It was deep and long and rumbled in your belly just as much as in your ears, and if you didn't know it was a friendly

lion in the cage you would have probably run in fright or been frozen to the spot in terror.

Charles hadn't roared that morning when they'd gone to see him. Fizz wondered if he would ever roar like that again: joyfully, full-throatedly.

He tried to push the thought out of his mind. He looked at the sea. Heard it roar again. 'I read a book once,' he said, hoping making conversation might stop him thinking sad thoughts, 'in the library, that said that *all* cats can swim.'

'Hmm,' Wystan said, unconvinced.

'No, really. They're actually pretty good at it,' Fizz went on, 'it's just most of them choose not to. It takes them ages to get their fur dry. It's such good-quality fur, you see, and they're a bit precious about it. Like to look their best all the time. Tigers though, they don't care, they look good wet or dry, I guess. They *love* to swim. In fact, this book said that you're more likely to get killed by a *tiger* when you're swimming than by a *shark*. Although I suppose,' he added as an afterthought, 'it probably depends on where you're doing the swimming.'

'In the tiger enclosure at the zoo?'

'More likely to be a tiger.'

'In the shark tank at the Aquarium?'

'More likely to be a shark.'

Wystan stopped walking. Fizz stopped too. (It only seemed polite.)

'Fizz?'

'Yes?'

'Why did you have to say that about the shark? I've got pictures in my head now.'

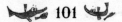

'Well, it was you that said about the shark tank and the Aquarium.'

'Yeah, and it was *you* that said about sharks *eating people*.'

Now Fizz was getting pictures in his head too. He'd been concentrating on the tigers. He got on well with big cats (or at least with Charles, who was the only one he knew), and although they were dangerous he had a good idea of how to be safe around them (keep on the outside of the bars, for instance), but now he had a shark swimming round in his head in a huge tank at an Aquarium just like the one they were walking towards, and Fizz had never learnt to swim. In his mind's eye he was splashing about desperately trying to learn (learning's a good thing, you usually know more at the end of it) and that huge fin was heading his way.

'They don't have sharks here, do they?' he said, trying to push the picture away with common sense and knowledge.

'I don't remember none,' Wystan answered, 'but that don't mean nothing. It was pretty boring in there and I weren't looking too close.'

'No, me neither. But . . . well, they would've been in with all the grey fish, wouldn't they? Right at the beginning?'

'I suppose. You're the one who knows stuff. You read books. Have you read what colour sharks might be?'

'I think . . .' said Fizz, racking his brains. 'I *think* they're all grey. Aren't they?'

'I guess we're gonna find out,' Wystan said glumly.

* * *

Just a minute or two later they were stood in front of the Aquarium. The glass doors at the front of the building were locked and, peering through them, they could see dim lights on inside. Grey shapes swam in tanks. Fizz hoped that none of them were sharks.

He hoped none of them were tigers either.

'Now,' he said, 'let's find a way in.'

CHAPTER SIX

In which some boys attempt to break
into an Aquarium and in which,
eventually, they do so

The boys skirted round the outside edge
of the Aquarium (not in real skirts,
which flap about in the wind and get caught
up in machinery, but in a metaphorical sense).

The plan was, instead of walking in through
the front door (which was locked anyway), to
sneak in round the side. When they were
watching the show that morning Fizz had

noticed that there was a place where the arena's wall dipped down low. He could see over it from his seat and out to sea. If they could make their way round the outside of the Aquarium to there, they'd be able to climb over. Then, from the pool, they could slip through the curtain that led backstage and find a door. Maybe, if they were really lucky, Fish might be in the pool when they got there, and they could all just slip back over the wall and away. Easy.

'Yeah, easy,' Wystan had grumbled sarcastically. But since he couldn't think of a better plan of his own, here he was, edging carefully.

To the seaward side of the Aquarium a path ran along beside the beach. Fizz had pointed at it, since it led the way they wanted to go, but as they'd rounded the corner it had narrowed. They had to walk in single file. Below them the waves splashed up and down the beach, crunching the hard shingle noisily.

They went as carefully as they could, the only light coming from the now vanished sun (which obviously didn't give them much light at all), and from the pale glow which shone from some windows high above them.

The path grew wetter and more slippery in the dark.

The concrete on their right seemed rougher, harder and colder. It spiked their hands with tiny sharp edges, but they had to touch it to make sure they weren't straying. They didn't want to slip and fall. It was a long drop to the beach, and the idea of crashing onto those hundreds of hard pebbles wasn't a happy one.

The spray from a big wave surrounded them like mist. The noise was deafening.

'Stop, stop, stop, stop,' whispered Fizz hurriedly.

Wystan bumped into his back.

Fizz wobbled, but didn't fall, gripping onto the rough concrete with one hand.

He felt in front of him with his foot. He had been right to stop. The path stopped too.

'Torch,' he said.

Wystan scrabbled around in his rucksack and handed the torch to Fizz.

In the circle of white light they saw where the path stopped. Just under Fizz's toes.

Shining the torch downwards, they could see the beach was further below them than they'd imagined. Ahead of them on their right the grey wall of the aquarium continued, rising up high above them like a castle wall. Some way in front, maybe twenty metres, maybe a bit more, the building got shorter, the wall lower.

'There,' said Fizz pointing into the distance. 'That's where we need to go, the wall comes right down. That's our way in.'

Wystan squinted. At that distance the beam of light from the torch was lost in the general

murk of the night, but Fizz was right, the wall was definitely getting lower. That must be the way to the pool.

'The path runs out,' he muttered through his beard. 'How we gonna get there?'

Fizz shone the light around his feet again. He pointed the torch just beyond the end of the path. There were big rocks piled up along the bottom of the wall. The tops of them were level with the path.

'Along there,' Fizz said. 'It'll be easy.'

'Easy?'

'Well, easier than clinging to the wall or learning to fly.'

Wystan couldn't argue with that. So he didn't.

Fizz lived in a circus. The circus is a place full of special skills and admirable bravery. He

hadn't spent his whole life putting his head in a lion's mouth every night. Sometimes he had had to help out with other acts too. He'd had a go at all sorts of things over the years.

He could juggle badly, he could ride a horse badly, he could make half- (but only half-) decent clown custard. He'd even done a bit of tightrope walking, though not on the high wire strung forty feet above the sawdust with no safety net. He'd learnt on the low wire, the one that wobbled a foot off the ground over an old mattress, that the acrobats used for practice.

He reckoned walking across the tops of those big boulders, piled up against the seawall of the Aquarium, would be a bit like that. Not so narrow of course, and with less sway underfoot and without anything to

soften the fall, but still, a little bit like walking the tightrope. A wet, lumpy, rock-hard
tightrope.

If only, he thought, he had been any good
at tightrope-walking. It had been another one
of those things he'd done badly.

Why didn't the way into the Aquarium
involve pouring custard into someone's trousers? He could do that. He could do that
pretty well. He knew just the right way to tip
the bucket, so it flowed smoothly, didn't just
clump out in one great splurge, but took its
time and luxuriated its way slowly down the
trouser legs. He knew just where to pour it in
so that both legs got filled evenly (there's
nothing worse than one custardy leg). He
even had a good idea of just how to run away
after you'd poured it: ideally at exactly the

moment *before* the one whose trousers are full of custard notices.

But, try as he might, he couldn't think how custard pouring could be of any use in this situation. Tricky tiptoe tightrope-like walking across the great dark wet sea boulders it was.

Fizz waited a few moments, listening to the constant repetitive surge and crash of the waves somewhere below him. The roar of them no longer reminded him of Charles, but of tigers and sharks (even though he knew they (sharks, I mean) don't roar), and his mind's eyes filled in the darkness with pictures of hungry beasts swimming round the foot of the rocks. *Oh, thank you, mind's eye*, he thought sarcastically.

Gathering his courage up in one super-sized bundle, he sat down on the edge of the path and lowered himself towards the first of the huge rocks. He touched it with his toe, gingerly (which considering the colour of his hair (red) was the way he touched most things), and then pushed himself upright.

He was standing on the stone. It curved under his feet and, although this may have been his imagination, it felt cold through the soles of his shoes.

Beneath him the vast dark sea crashed up the beach and round the rocks. It seemed even louder now. A mist of spray whooshed up at him, and then the crunching shuckling sound roared to itself as the waves dragged the shingle backwards, back towards the deep water.

Nevertheless, Fizz stood firm. He stood strong. He stood brave. He was coming to find his friend, he had goodness on his side, how could he fail?

He waved the torch in front of him, trying to work out his next move, how to get to the next rock, how to pick his way, boulder by boulder, along to the Aquarium's arena and their only way in.

The top of the next rock looked miles away. He gathered himself up to make the jump . . .

Now, I feel I must interject here, just briefly. Normally, as you know, I sit quiet in the corner over there (imagine me pointing into a corner), typing the words out, telling Fizz's story as best I can and keeping all my opinions to myself. You know I don't like to get involved or get in the way of the story; that's not my

job. My job is just to share Fizzlebert's adventures with you as straightforwardly as I can. I don't meddle. I don't fiddle. I don't make stuff up. I don't tell you what I think or ramble on about biscuits and suchlike; I simply recount what happened. Just the facts, ma'am. That's all.

However, I can't keep quiet any more.

I must speak up.

I have to say this.

If I don't, then I won't be able to sleep at night, worrying what might happen.

Here goes.

What Fizz and Wystan are doing is *utterly stupid*. It's crazy. It's ridiculous. But more than that, it's dangerous.

Climbing over giant sea rocks is bad enough under normal circumstances. They're damp, they're covered in slime, they're hard and slippery. You could fall and break your leg, your arm, your neck even. You could drown in a poorly placed rockpool with a faceful of angry sea anemones. You will almost certainly be attacked by crabs.

It's dangerous even when you've got people nearby looking out for you. At least they can ring for the coastguard and the air ambulance when you slip. But nobody knows where Fizz and Wystan are, they're on a *secret* mission. If they fall, they'll be stuck, alone, damp, and nipped by crabs. Possibly nipped to death.

Not only that, but what if they fell and got swept out to sea by the surging incoming tide with its treacherous undertows and ensnaring weeds? There are still crabs under the water, you know.

I can only ask, 'What on earth is he thinking?'

Add to all that the fact that they're doing this mountaineering nonsense *in the dark*, and this really is not a Good Thing.

It's an adventure, for sure. And this book wouldn't be very interesting if there wasn't *some* sort of adventure in it. But it's a *stupid* adventure.

I'm not saying Fizz is stupid, because he's not. He's a good kid and his heart's in the right place. He's doing this all to save his best friend, Fish, and that's a Good Thing, it shows he's listening to the commands of his heart, and that's important. But what I *am* saying is that sometimes the heart disagrees with the head, and at those times it's important to remember that your head is the more sensible

 118

of the two, being the one that has a brain in it. Your heart is just a squishy pump that moves blood around your body, and it only works if you keep the blood on the inside. So, please, please, please: listen to your head.

I just wanted to say that, you know, get it out there. So, now, if anyone copies Fizz's stupid antics and is eaten by crabs, I can at least point to this bit and say, 'I did warn them,' and no one can pin your accidents on me. Let's make this clear: your stupid acts are *your* stupid acts. (And mine are mine, but let's not talk about those.)

'Hey, Fizz,' said Wystan. 'Look!'

'What?' said Fizz, trying to keep his balance as he turned the torch on his bearded companion. His heart was beating so hard in his chest he could hardly hear Wystan over the noise of it.

 119

His bearded friend was pointing his torch at the Aquarium wall just above his head.

'Someone's left a window open,' he said. 'Shall we climb in here?'

Fizz looked down at the great, weedy, damp rock he was standing on, and the long fall either side of it, and then up at the open window, thought for a very short moment, and said, 'Yeah, okay.'

Wystan reached out and helped Fizz back up onto the path.

Without talking, Wystan interlocked his fingers and lowered his entwined hands down to about the height of his knees. Fizz put one of his feet in them and in the age-old tradition of the bunk-up, Wystan bunked him up.

Fizz's hands got a grip on the window frame and he pulled himself in. Once on the window sill, he lowered his legs into the darkness behind him. To his relief he found a platform which took his weight.

He leant out the window and caught the rucksack Wystan threw up to him.

'Do you need me to lower the rope?' Fizz asked.

'Nah, don't bother about that,' said Wystan. 'Just stick your hands out.'

Wystan crouched and sprang like a boy trained in acrobatics and with several years of circus experience under his belt. He caught hold of Fizz's arms and, with a painful yank, swung himself up over Fizz's head and through the window so that he landed with a professional acrobat's crash somewhere on the floor.

Well, at last, they were in, and I think we've all earned a cup of tea and a break. Well done everybody, take five minutes to relax.

CHAPTER SEVEN

In which some purple fish are seen
and in which a conversation about
pink sharks is had

Fizzlebert pointed the torch at his feet.

He was standing on a toilet seat lid.

'Wystan?' he called in a whisper, waving the torch around the room. 'Are you okay?'

'Yeah, nothing broken,' said his bearded accomplice.

Fizz found him with the torch. His beard was spilling out around his chin like a comet's black furry tail. In the torchlight it threw weird shadows on the wall.

'Well, we're in. Now we've got to try to find Fish. Where's the door?'

'Here, look.'

Wystan pointed and his finger touched it. It really was quite a small room they'd climbed into. You might say, it was the smallest room. But then again, you might just call it the loo, and that would be fine too.

Fizz opened the door a crack. The corridor outside was lit by widely-spaced, dimly glowing lights in the ceiling. The walls along either side were filled, to no one's great surprise, by tanks of water.

The boys turned their torches off.

'Look at this,' Wystan said, looking into a nearby tank.

'Shark?' asked Fizz, nervously.

'Nah, just little purple things. And they're all still swimming about.'

Indeed they were, fishy little purple shapes, like pipe-cleaners with nozzle-like snouts and tiny frilly fins halfway down their backs. They swished about in the water, rushing between waving fronds of weeds as if they were chasing one another in a miniature unending game of tag.

'What did you expect?' asked Fizz, looking in the tank himself.

'I thought they'd be asleep,' said Wystan. 'It's getting late.'

'Oh Wystan, Wystan, Wystan,' Fizz said, shaking his head like Dr Surprise. 'If you read the label here,' (he pointed at the label by the side of the tank that he'd just read), 'you'll see that these fish are from Australia.'

'So?'

'What time it is in Australia?'

'Same time as anywhere else?'

'Australia's on the other side of the world. So, instead of being half past eight at night, it's actually half past eight in the morning there.'

'Really?

'And that means that *these* fish have probably just woken up. They're chasing each other because they've just had their breakfast and are full of energy. For them, it's just the beginning of another day.'

Wystan muttered something into his beard that Fizz couldn't make out.

'Dad's aunt Sycamore moved to Australia years ago. She sends us letters every now and then and they've *always* got the wrong time written at the top. And the wrong day, too. But it's only the wrong time for *us*; for her and everyone else in Australia, and these fish, it's right.'

Wystan gave Fizz another of his looks over the top of his beard. This one meant something like, 'I'm not sure I believe anything you've just said, but I'm not going to argue with you right now because that would just take up precious time that could be used searching for our missing sea lion.' (Wystan had very expressive eyes.)

'So,' Fizz said, taking Wystan's hint, 'which way?'

The bearded boy pointed to the left, down the corridor, further into the Aquarium.

They tiptoed past tank after tank after tank of purple fish. Some were small like the pipe-cleaner fish they'd already seen, and some were huge fat things that hung in the middle of their tanks, floating like lumpy balloons, staring at the boys with ugly pudgy eyes. They opened and closed their mouths as if they kept remembering something important to say and then forgetting it before they said it.

To Fizz's relief none of them looked remotely shark-like.

Every now and then they passed one of those empty tanks, looking lonely among all the slowly swimming sea-life on either side, with a pasted-on sign saying things like STOLEN FISH: REWARD OFFERED or HAVE YOU SEEN THIS FISH: MISSING SINCE SUNDAY NIGHT?

Hundreds of fishy eyes, small and large, black and yellow and red and orange, followed the boys as they walked. Occasionally the fish were extra interested and swam along in their tanks keeping pace with the boys until they swam head-first into the wall. Being fish of very little brain, they forgot Fizz and Wystan immediately and simply swam back the way they'd come, wondering where this headache

had come from. (Had Unnecessary Sid, one of the more irritating clowns in the circus, been there, he would have made an awful 'haddock' joke, because 'haddock' sounds a bit like 'headache', and that's his idea of fun. Luckily he wasn't (he was at a different 'plaice'), so we don't have to listen to him 'carp' on.)

When they reached the end of the purple corridor, Fizz peered round the corner into another corridor of fish tanks.

This new corridor glimmered palely pink, like an underwater grotto a nine-year-old mermaid has been allowed to decorate all by herself. The sparse light from the ceiling reflected off the thousands of scales of the assembled pink fish swimming in their little glassy worlds lined along the walls.

'At least there ain't gonna be any sharks in here,' Wystan whispered.

'Why's that?' Fizz whispered back.

'You're not gonna find a pink shark, are you? Pink's the most girly colour of all, and sharks ain't *girly* fish, are they?'

'Well,' said Fizz, pondering the matter deeply, 'I think *some* sharks must be girls.'

Fizz wished he'd read a book about sharks when he'd last been at the library. There were, he knew, some weird sharks out there. He couldn't remember any pink sharks, though he'd seen a picture of a hammerhead shark, whose head is, as you probably know, shaped like a hammer. (They don't often keep hammerhead sharks in aquariums because they're always smashing the glass. Once they've broken out, they lie on the

131

floor, flapping about with their great rough sandpapery tails and weird-shaped heads, until someone comes along and puts them in a new tank. It's very annoying.)

'Fizz,' Wystan said, interrupting my almost entirely true anecdote about hammerhead sharks.

He pointed at a sign on the wall. It said TO THE ARENA.

The boys looked at each other and grinned. That was where they wanted to get. That was where they'd last seen Fish, during the afternoon's show. They followed the sign's pointing finger and hurried along the corridor. Everything was going to plan.

There were loads of pink fish swimming around on either side as they ran. If you want to skip back and read the description of the purple fish a few pages ago but change the word 'purple' to the word 'pink' then you'll get a pretty good idea of what it looked like. I don't want to upset any fish fans, any collectors of tropical beauties, or anyone with a pressed fish collection in their rainy-day drawer, but I really can't think of anything else to say about them. They were pink, they swam, and they could breathe underwater. That's it. I challenge you to make an Aquarium more interesting than that. In fact, here's a blank page for you to have a go.

During that blank page the boys stopped running.

They'd heard the sound of footsteps heading towards them. Clumping footsteps, and the jangle of a chain or a key ring. And the sound of someone whistling. To be precise, someone whistling, 'What shall we do with the drunken sailor'.

Fizz's first thought was the same as Wystan's first thought: *Admiral Spratt-Haddock!*

Their matching second thoughts were: *Run the other way!*

Putting the plan in action straight away, they ran back the way they'd come, as quietly as they could but also as quickly, down the pink corridor. They darted down the first opening they saw into yet another corridor, this time filled with the shimmering green

light that reflected off shimmering green fish. And there they skidded to a halt for a second time. They weren't alone. Ten feet in front of them was a man.

In that moment Fizz's heart couldn't decide whether to freeze solid or jump out of his chest and run off by itself. Instead it fluttered like a bird behind his ribs. They were caught!

But no, he saw, it wasn't quite so bad. They'd not been seen. His heart breathed a sigh of relief. They weren't safe yet, but it could be worse.

The figure had its back to them. It was crouched in the middle of the corridor, dressed all in black, with a long coat that hung to the ground, and seemed to be manhandling something into an inside pocket. There was a puddle of water around its feet and a long pole with a net by its side.

Behind them the footsteps were still slowly heading in their direction (whoever it was hadn't heard them running, or they'd be hurrying faster), and the whistling was growing louder.

The mysterious stranger in front of them suddenly looked over his shoulder. Fizz couldn't see his face because he was wearing a black balaclava (which is a bit like a badly knitted woolly hat), but the two peering red eyes that burned out from the woollen blank blackness made him gulp in fear.

'You?' the figure hissed, keeping his voice down and looking around him. 'What on earth are you doing here? Did *he* send you?'

Fizzlebert didn't know what to say. His dad had asked him not to talk to strangers, and this man looked pretty strange. His coat was flapping, as if there were something writhing around inside it and water was dripping from it to the floor.

'Pah,' the man spat, when Fizz couldn't muster an answer, and waved his hand dismissively. 'I don't care. You're on your own, kids. Better *you* get caught than me, eh? I'm outta here.'

The voice rasped in the damp aquarium air and if Fizz hadn't been standing beside Wystan he might've given a little squeak of fear at the unkindness, the venom, the distaste the words seemed filled with.

The stranger turned on his heels and ran, away from the boys and from the approaching footsteps and jingling keys. In a second he was gone, vanished round the next corner.

'What was that all about?' Wystan asked in a low voice.

'I don't know,' Fizz replied, thoroughly unnerved by the episode.

The whistling footsteps sounded like they were just about to come round the corner behind them.

Wystan grabbed Fizz's arm and hissed a hurried, 'Run!'

They set off down the corridor themselves, following the stranger, needing to run to get away from the footsteps behind them, but not wanting to run so fast that they caught up with the weird man in front. It made the whole experience even more scary. Two ways to get caught, and which would be worse?

Just before they reached the corner the masked man had nipped round twenty seconds earlier, Fizz spotted a door on their left labelled *Keep Out*.

'Here!' he whispered urgently, skidding to a halt.

He yanked the door open and they both bundled in, closing it as quickly, but as quietly, as they could behind them.

The two boys huddled together in the dark, holding their breaths as the sound of the whistling continued to draw closer and closer until it was almost upon them, just like the end of the chapter.

CHAPTER EIGHT

In which a night-watchman is met and
in which a sandwich is
inconvenienced

Fizz and Wystan looked around the room.
In one corner a TV was showing a programme about aquariums. It was shot in fuzzy black and white and showed corridor after corridor of fish tanks. It flicked between them, always from the same high angle, which meant you could hardly see any fish. It seemed, for the few seconds Fizz watched it,

a very odd and probably boring programme. (But then again, he had hardly ever watched television, being too busy circussing, so he didn't know if this was as good as it got, or if there were better programmes available.)

The glow from the TV lit the room with a flickering grey light. There was a desk. On it was a sandwich, still wrapped in cling-film, and a steaming cup of coffee. It looked like someone was due back any minute. By the side of the desk a kettle rested precariously on top of a pile of magazines.

There was a revolving chair and in the corner of the room, beside a filing cabinet, sat a bucket with half a dozen upended mops leant in it. A coat hung on a hook and a calendar hung on a different hook. It had a picture of a shark (a grey one), jaws open, lurching out of the water at a cameraman. The caption said, 'Smile, please!'

What the room lacked, importantly, was another door. Fizz counted twice just to be sure.

'One.'

'One.'

And, just to be clear, the door he counted was the door they'd just come in through. The one with the whistling outside it.

The door handle rattled as whoever was out in the corridor took hold of it.

The boys looked around again, desperately hoping to spot a hiding place they hadn't noticed the first time they'd looked round desperately.

Under the desk? What if the person outside sat down to eat their sandwich?

Behind the mops? There wasn't much room. Even half a dozen mops are quite thin.

Under the coat? Not only would your legs stick out, but Wystan's beard would poke round the edges.

In the telly? That was just stupid.

There must be somewhere. There must be, there must be, Fizz thought.

The boys watched, eyes glued in fear, as the door handle started to turn. They were caught. They were done for. They'd be made to walk the plank, fed to the fish, or at the very least have the police phoned on them. And then . . .

And then a telephone rang. On the other side of the door.

The handle sprang back up to its closed position as the person outside let go. The

phone stopped ringing and a woman's voice answered it.

'I'm at work, honey. You shouldn't . . . They're in the cupboard by the microwave. . . . No, not the blue bottle, that's . . . Just take two, and then . . .' and so on.

When the telephone call ended, the speaker finally opened the door, switched on the light and stepped into a cosy little room. She looked around and saw it was filled with a TV and a desk and a sandwich and a coat and a cup of coffee and a calendar and some mops and absolutely no boys at all.

Mrs Darling took her hat off and hung it on the coat-rack above her coat. It was the peaked hat of a security guard and she wore the white shirt, dark blue jacket and trousers to match.

She had short blonde hair, shaped just the same as her hat until she ran her hand through it, after which it looked like what her mother had used to call 'a mess'. But it was short, and messy short hair is neater than uncombed long hair, so she was still smart enough to not look out of place in her uniform. Her eyes were brown and big, always on the lookout, and her nose interrupted the spatter of freckles that covered her cheeks. She was tall and not what you'd call thin. She wasn't fat either, but muscle-y. Not as muscle-y as Fizz's dad, of course, but she lifted small weights in her spare time. There was a tattoo of an oyster on her left bicep. (She'd asked for a mussel, but the tattoo-ist didn't know his shellfish very well.)

As she sat down at the desk she yawned widely. Although it was almost nine o'clock at night it was still early in the day for her. She worked the night shift at the Aquarium and, like those purple Australian fish, her day was all upside down.

She glanced at the TV monitor. The screen showed her what was happening elsewhere in the building. Every few seconds it flicked to a different camera in one of the many Aquarium corridors. She'd be spending most of the night sat looking at it. Sometimes she'd go out and walk around. Then she'd come back and look at the screen a bit more. That was her job. Guarding the fish. And do you know what?

Nothing *ever* happened.

Well, not until a week ago. After a whole year of sitting up at night watching nothing but fish bobbing about in their tanks, finally

something had started going on. She felt a mix of excitement and embarrassment at the thought of it.

The fish had started going missing. They were being stolen from under her very nose. The pattern was the same, every night. One of the cameras would stop working, and by the time she'd found out which corridor it was and gone to check it out the thief would be gone, along with some of the Admiral's prized fish.

What made it all the more embarrassing for her was that she couldn't work out how the burglar was getting in. The main doors were always locked when she checked them, and she never found a broken window or door anywhere else. It was a mystery.

But on the previous nights the robberies

had happened well after midnight. She looked at her watch. Right now it wasn't even nine o'clock. She had some time to kill. So she reached under the desk and pulled a thick book out of her bag. It was a murder mystery with a gruesome cover and well-thumbed pages. (Maybe, she thought, if she paid close enough attention to the policeman in the book, she might get some tips for putting an end to the fish-napping.)

Putting her feet up on the desk and taking one last look at the TV screen, she leant back in her chair, opened her book, tucked the bookmark away in her inside pocket and began to read.

After a minute she reached out and picked up her coffee cup. Took a sip. Put it back down. She didn't take her eyes off the book.

It was just getting to a good bit. She turned the page. Drank some more coffee. Turned another page.

She came to the end of a chapter and put the bookmark in its place and put the book down. She yawned again and reached out for her sandwich.

Her fingers touched the cling-film and she stopped. There was something wrong. She'd made herself a big sandwich, full of salad and

ham and pickle and cheese. What her fingers were touching didn't quite feel right, so she did what any highly trained security guard (she had a certificate and everything) would do in such a situation: she looked at the sandwich. What she saw surprised her so much she said a word I'm not going to share.

Her sandwich had been trodden on.

Let's rewind five minutes.

You know when Wystan and Fizzlebert wanted to hide and there didn't seem to be anywhere to hide? Well, here's what happened . . .

'We're stuck,' Wystan whispered. 'The game's up.'

Fizz could hear his heart beating in his chest. It was thumping too loud. It was going too fast.

He felt like he was trapped in one of those dreams where you're in a small office-cum-broom cupboard in an Aquarium you're not meant to be in and someone's about to open the door and find you. Almost exactly like that dream.

He ran his hand through his unruly hair and then, to his joy and surprise, spotted something.

'Look at that,' he said, grabbing Wystan's sleeve.

They looked at the ceiling. They hadn't looked at it before. Why would they? It was just a ceiling. But it was made of those rectangular panels, resting on a sort of metal grid. The panels were made of, what? Foam board or something? They weren't heavy, Fizz could guess that much.

He got Wystan to stand on the desk, and in a flash he was up on Wystan's shoulders pushing a tile up and to the side.

He poked his head through the hole and looked around.

In amongst the wires and pipes and dust, there was a metal walkway. It ran above the fish tanks. He grabbed hold of the struts and, with a little jiggling, pulled himself up and onto it.

Wystan, with one acrobatic leap, grab and flip, wasn't far behind him.

'The panel,' Fizz hissed, pointing.

Wystan quickly shoved the rectangular piece of board back into the hole and the boys were left sitting still and safe in the dark.

Below them they heard the door open and close and then a click as the person switched on the light.

Had the ceiling tile slotted back into place properly the boys would have been sat safe and snug in the dark, but in their hurry it had ended up at a slightly skew angle. A shaft of light from the office, like the beam of a torch or a spotlight in the circus ring, pushed up into the darkness.

They didn't dare move. Even shifting to get comfortable set the metal walkway they were lying on rattling and creaking.

The two boys were safe, they felt, but they were still trapped. They just had to hope that whoever was down there didn't decide to look up.

A long minute went by.

Mrs Darling looked up.

She immediately noticed the out-of-place

roof tile, because she was specially trained to be observant of things that were out of place.

'At last,' she said to herself under her breath, 'I've got you.'

She slid open the desk drawer as quietly as she could and pulled out a torch that was attached to a length of elastic. She put it on her head, like you would a hat, and switched the torch on. She looked around the room and everywhere she looked she saw the circle of torchlight ahead of her.

Then, moving as carefully as she could, she climbed onto her desk herself, taking care not to tread on her sandwich, because the imprint of the culprit's shoe might be important evidence later on.

She pushed the panel out of the way and stood up.

She wasn't sure what it was she was seeing at first.

Her first impression was that there were two boys up on the walkway, but then she thought there was a man and a boy. Then it struck her that if it was a man it was a short one, so maybe a boy and a dwarf. And then she thought, *if one of them's a dwarf, maybe they're both dwarfs.* And then she thought, *I'd best just get them because whoever they are or whatever they are, they've been nicking the Admiral's fish.*

She reached out and grabbed hold of one of their ankles.

She hoped that would be enough to stop them, but it wasn't. Whoever's ankle she'd grabbed kicked her loose and the two trespassers began running.

She hauled herself up and gave chase.

CHAPTER NINE

In which a chase is made and in
which a boy gets wet

Fizzlebert ran like his life depended on it,
as if there were a tiger behind him (or a
shark (with legs)). He didn't know where he
was running, but he ran there anyway. Behind
him he could hear Wystan doing the same.

The metal walkway was narrow and they
ran in single file. It wobbled and clanged with
every step, the sound echoing strangely off the

water below them. Fizz had been furthest from the security guard when she'd made a grab for them and so he was the one leading the way.

They were running across the tops of the fish tanks. Off to his left he could see a sea of ceiling tiles and bundles of wires and pipes running this way and that, but beneath the walkway the tops of the fish tanks were all open to the air. Water lapped and light from the corridor beyond the tanks' glass rippled up through the water, casting an eerie light across the concrete ceiling above his head.

If he'd had time to pause, lean on the railing and look down for a minute he would have seen the little faces of fish poke out of the water wondering what all the commotion in the sky was. But he didn't have time to stop and look.

Up ahead both the rattling walkway and the row of tanks seemed to stop: there was a brick wall and, just before that, the top rungs of a ladder leading down to who knew where. He slowed down. He didn't want to run full pelt and jump off the end into the unknown. Wystan probably would've, he thought, but Wystan was an acrobat, he did that sort of thing. Fizz stuck his head in a lion's mouth. That was a useful skill, he was sure, but it didn't prepare you for a chase like this and a jump like that.

The thumping footsteps behind him grew faster, the rattling louder. His heart was pounding in his chest and his lungs were straining with all the pumping in and out he was asking them to do.

As he slowed down he felt Wystan close behind him, and heard him shout, 'Faster!'

Fizz realised that Wystan couldn't see the end coming and didn't know why he needed to slow down. So he half-turned, meaning to shout an explanation over his shoulder, and Wystan banged into him and they both tripped over one another's feet and went tumbling.

Fizz hit the wet floor beyond the end of the fish tanks with a hard *crump*. There was a great deep splash behind him and a spray of water, like a heavy but incredibly short indoor rainstorm, landed on him and on the floor around him.

A second went by before Fizz tried moving. He hadn't hurt himself: his thick Ringmaster's coat had absorbed the fall and he'd covered his head with his arms. Nothing was broken, all his limbs were working and though he'd have some bruises to show come the morning, he was able to stand up and move about.

Above him he heard shouting and splashing.

Wystan must have rolled to the side when he tripped, slipped under the railings and fallen off the walkway into the last of the fish tanks. Fizz didn't know if Wystan could swim or not, but the tanks weren't that deep or big, and with a beard like that, surely he'd float face upwards?

Fizz had to make a choice. He could go back up the ladder and get caught with his friend. Or he could run through the door in the wall in front of him, while the guard was busy dealing with Wystan's brilliant, self-sacrificing distraction.

Fizz looked up at the ladder, up at the ceiling where the weird watery light played in rippling ribbons, and hoped that his friend would understand.

When he got the chance, he'd come back for Wystan. He'd see if he could rescue Fish and Wystan both, although he didn't know how he could do it.

He grabbed the handle of the door, turned it and stepped out into the cool air of the evening.

Up in the sky stars twinkled and the sea was crashing somewhere nearby.

He was in a little concrete courtyard that smelt of fish. In the middle of the wall on his right hung a curtain, rustling softly in the light breeze that moved the smell of fish around the small square.

He knew where he was. He was backstage. That curtain led out to the pool he'd been aiming for. At last he felt his luck was turning.

The best thing about backstage (he knew this from the circus where the Ringmaster was always complaining) was that it was full of *stuff*. And *stuff* was exactly what he needed right now. Moving quickly he dragged some empty crates in front of the door, and then piled some rope, two buckets and a long pole with a net on the end on top of them. It wouldn't keep the door shut for long, not if someone *really* wanted to get through, but it was better than nothing, and the noise of all that lot crashing to the ground would at least give him some warning.

Breathing a little easier, he finally felt able to continue his search.

If he could find Fish before that security guard found *him*, then he'd be able to prove that he and Wystan had done the right thing breaking into the Aquarium. When everyone saw that Spratt-Haddock had kidnapped the circus's sea lion, well, he wouldn't have a leg to stand on.

So first, Fizz asked himself, where would a sea lion be at this time of the evening?

He was sure he wouldn't be anywhere indoors, in one of those tanks. Fish preferred to sleep outside. He had his paddling pool and he'd lie on the grass with his tail in it, gently splashing about, while he snored loud fishy snores into the night.

He wasn't here in the courtyard, so he must be beside the pool.

Fizz carefully parted the curtain and poked his head through. Across the water, which rippled brightly under the white floodlights, he could see the seats where they'd been sitting earlier that day watching the show. There was no one there now. And it wasn't just that there were no people there, Fizz couldn't see Fish anywhere either.

More worrying was what he *could* see. Waving into his view, inches in front of his face, was a long curved silver hook, which was attached to the arm and body (and head and legs) of Admiral Spratt-Haddock himself.

And if that's not the cue for a chapter break, then I'm writing the wrong book.

CHAPTER TEN

In which Wystan gets wet and in
which Fizz makes an escape

Wystan Barboozul, the bearded boy,
fell.

It seemed to take an age, but it could only
have been a split second before he hit the
water and the world abruptly changed. From
one of dry warm airiness, it flipped in an
instant to one of wet cold wateriness. He
thrashed around, kicking with his legs, trying

to find out which way was up. His beard spread out around him curling like black inky tentacles.

Wystan had never learnt to swim. He had a paddle sometimes, when Fish wanted company in his paddling pool, but he couldn't lie down in it and even if he could have, swimming lengths would have been far too easy, since the pool was probably only three inches longer than he was.

That wasn't to say Wystan had *never* tried to learn to swim, but he had been banned from the one public swimming pool he'd been to because of his beard. (He had refused to wear a chin cap and there had been mean-spirited complaints from other children's parents. Apparently he'd looked so scary with the bedraggled beard floating out from his face across the water like black wriggling furry fingers that a girl called Sandra Loosley had wet herself, right there in the water. The whole place had to be emptied and refilled with clean water, which took hours.)

So, for years and years Wystan hadn't been swimming, hadn't had a chance to try it, and now, all of a sudden and rather unexpectedly, he was having a splash course.

And guess what? It turned out to be easy. There was enough air trapped in his beard that he floated, head above the water. As he kicked his legs about, he found that he moved forwards. He tried moving his hands too. He moved even quicker. This was a piece of cake, he said to himself, even going so far as to imagine what sort of cake (Battenberg).

The only problems he found were that the

water was rather cold and the tank he was in wasn't quite big enough. As far as fish tanks went, it was a big one, much bigger than some that they'd seen that evening, but as far as swimming pools went, it was tiny. He was already up against the glass. He'd have to turn around and swim the other way now.

And then he remembered how he'd got where he was: the break in, the hiding, the chase, Fizz, Fish! Funny how a plunge in cold water had flushed it all out of his head for a moment. Well, he thought, he'd better find his way out of the tank and get on with the search for their sea lion.

Paddling his hands and treading water with his feet, he slowly revolved.

It was only as he did this that it occurred to him to wonder what lived in the fish tank.

Whose home was he floating in? Who might be watching his feet waving around in their back garden?

And then he saw something that would have upset Sandra Loosley greatly. There was a fin in the water.

No, that's wrong. There was a fin poking *out of* the water.

There was no need to worry about a fin, of course. A fin never hurt anyone. It was what was *attached to* the fin, *in* the water that was worrying Wystan. *I'm pretty sure it's not a tiger,* his brain said, *they don't have fins. But if it isn't a tiger, then it must be . . .*

It was coming towards him. It was gliding through the water in his direction. And although it had a pinkish shade to it, it also had a decidedly sharkish shape.

He pedalled his feet and flailed his hands about desperately, somehow hoping that would boost him out of the water and into the air. It didn't. Instead it just sprayed water up and hid the approaching fin from view.

Wystan didn't not see the fin for very long, because as soon as he stopped splashing his hands about it was back, and so much closer, and what was worse it seemed to be moving faster, towards him. But then . . . then it vanished, it sank out of sight and the tank was calm again. The shark had gone. Had he scared it off? *Oh wow*, he thought, *I scared off a shark, wait till I tell Fizz about this . . .*

The biggest pinkest set of tooth-filled jaws Wystan had ever seen burst out of the water directly in front of him, huge and pink and gaping, and they slammed shut just as something grabbed his collar, and then he was going upwards, hauled up like luggage on an elastic band, and *thump!* he was lying on his back on the metal walkway, dripping water back into the tank below.

Wystan breathed a sigh of relief, a big one, and even as Mrs Darling said, 'Oh goodness! I've caught the burglar!', he leaned over and watched the great murky pink shape of a shark circling below him, trailing wisps of black hair from the side of its mouth.

He felt his beard. Even in its wet, bedraggled state he could tell it was now lopsided.

Fizz pulled his head back through the curtains as quick as he could.

Admiral Spratt-Haddock was standing on the poolside stage with his back to the curtain. Fizz had seen him, but he hadn't seen Fizz.

'Listen, me lovelies,' said the Admiral's salty voice. He clearly wasn't talking to Fizz, which meant there must be other people out there. 'Swabs has sent us a copy of the evening paper. He said we'd be mighty interested in something on page 23. Shall we have us a look then, me hearties?'

There was a rustle of newspaper pages being turned.

'Here it is!' the Admiral exclaimed. He cleared his throat with a tarry 'ahem' before reading out what Fizz quickly realised was a review. '*All can agree that Admiral Spratt-Haddock's once wonderful 'Quarium has been going down-hill* . . . mumble, mumble. I'll just skip ahead a bit, here we go . . . *but now it seems a corner has been turned. Take a seat in the arena and prepare for the show of a lifetime.*' Although the Admiral's voice had sunk at the beginning of the review, when he reached the words 'show of a life-time', energy sprang back into his throat. 'Did you hear that?' he shouted, with a saucy cackle. '*Show of a lifetime!* Not bad, eh?' He muttered his way through the next few lines before saying clearly, '*The sea lion, Pescado, the 'Quarium's*

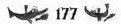

latest star, is both funny and touching: a brilliant comedian, an astonishing acrobat and, as you'd expect, an accomplished swimmer. Wherever the Admiral found this wily, winsome, witty beast, I recommend he go back and find some more. For once, a show worth seeing. Three stars.'

The newspaper made the noise of a newspaper being folded away and stuffed in a nautical chap's coat's large pocket.

'Three stars!' the Admiral shouted. 'That's amazing, astonishing, wonderful! A show worth seeing! She said you were brilliant, Pescado, my shipmate. Oh, you were so right to come aboard when you did! I saw your talent straight off, didn't I? Me old sea lion, me old first mate!' A small burst of maniacal laughter from the Admiral. 'I've got a nose for talent. Remember, I was there when they caught the great Cedric the Swordfish? Old Frank had him down for supper, but I made him a star!' The Admiral's voice fell so low, Fizz had to press his ear against the curtain to hear him. '. . . stupid fish. How could I know those eels were live? I'm not an electrician, am I? But Pescado, my dear boy, my lubber, my star! That's all behind me now. You've put us back on the map. You've breathed new life into our salt-caked, salt-baked lungs. Go on, give us a kiss!'

There was a barking honk, which sounded like a reply.

It didn't just sound like a reply, it sounded like Fish replying.

That must be who he's talking to, Fizz thought. He'd wondered why he hadn't heard anyone else saying anything. Like a Ringmaster, the Admiral was talking to his acts. Fish would be out there, and maybe Philip the otter, and the pool would probably be filled with all the fish artistes.

So, Fizz had the Admiral just where he wanted him, and Fish within his reach. He was fizzing with excitement. Now was the time to make his move, to put his brand new plan into action.

He was about to burst through the curtain, push the Admiral into the pool and shout for Fish to follow him, when a new voice appeared on the scene.

'Ahoy there, Admiral! I've caught a burglar, sir! I've got him. Look! Look!'

'What?' shouted the salty fiend.

'Over here, Admiral.'

'Mrs Darling? Who's that?'

'It's an intruder, sir. I pulled him out of the

shark tank, just now. There was another one, but it got away.'

'What is it?'

'I think,' she said, carefully, 'it's a boy.'

'But, that thing on its face, it looks like . . .'

'It's a disguise, Admiral. I tried pulling it off, but it's stuck on with glue.'

'It's *not* a disguise,' Wystan's voice snapped.

'A bearded boy?' Mrs Darling said. 'Who's ever heard of such a thing?'

'Aha,' said Admiral Spratt-Haddock, his voice cold. '*I've* heard of such a thing. I've heard of such a thing just recently. Where'd'ya find the furry fiend?'

'I fished him out of the shark tank, sir. He'd fallen in whilst running away.'

'The shark tank? Which one?'

'Austrian blushing shark, sir.'

'Nasty. You got him out whole?'

'Yes sir. And I thought I'd best show him to you first, sir, before I phoned the police.'

'Police?' the Admiral said, slowly, rubbing his chin with his hook. 'Methinks there's no need for that. I can deal with this one meself. Just one little shrimp? And me an Admiral and all? Oh, you leave it to me, Mrs Darling.' The Admiral chuckled wickedly.

'Ahem. *Two* intruders, sir.'

'Two intruders? Oh aye, you said. Another boy?'

'I *think* it was a boy,' Mrs Darling offered, 'but I didn't get a good look at him. This one's playing dumb. They were scuttling around up in the gangways, looking to scoop themselves more of your fish, I'd say. I was too busy heaving this one out of the shark tank to see where the other got to.'

'Well, Mrs Darling, you'd best get back to the search, and leave this dear little bearded urchin with me. And, Mrs Darling . . .'

'Yes, Admiral?'

'Lock them doors behind you.'

'Aye aye, Admiral.'

As soon as Fizz heard the door on the other side of the pool swing shut, he put his earlier plan (which wasn't much of a plan, but was all he had), now slightly modified to take account of the change in circumstances (push the Admiral in the pool, rescue Fish *and* Wystan, escape somehow), into action.

'Arrgghhh!' he shouted as he burst out through the curtain, pushing the surprised Admiral straight into the deep pool . . .

. . . except . . .

. . . the Admiral had moved and Fizz found

he was pushing nothing, nothing but air, and the thing about pushing air is that air doesn't push back, and so Fizz went flying, for the second time in ten minutes.

He fell, arms whirling like skinny feather-less wings, straight into the next chapter.

CHAPTER ELEVEN

In which Fizz gets wet and in which
an Admiral is questioned

Fizzlebert Stump fell.

Wystan Barboozul shouted.

And Admiral Spratt-Haddock lunged with
his hook.

Fizz's beautiful red Ringmaster's coat
caught on the steel spike, and he dangled for
a moment in the air before he slipped out of
the coat and fell again, this time straight down

into the pool, crashing into the water with a flailing, panicked splash. His coat swayed forlornly from the Admiral's hook.

Fizz, having neither a beard nor a swimming instructor to hand, suddenly remembered he couldn't swim. (There was a shower in the caravan, but he avoided that as much as he could.)

The water was cold, shockingly so, and Fizz's breath exploded out of his body (through his mouth) as he hit it. Under the water all he could see were bubbles, whirling round him. He didn't know which way was up and which was down. He couldn't tell if moving his arms or legs was having any effect, but he threw them about anyway, just in case.

He had the distinct feeling, in the pit of his stomach, that he was sinking. He was going

down. After years of putting his head in a lion's mouth, was this the way things would end? Drowning while attempting to push a pirate into a pool? He imagined what his mum would say: 'Drowning in custard I understand, but *water*? Why didn't he just drink it?'

Then he thought he could see light somewhere, and sparkles somewhere off beyond the bubble clouds, and then a sudden huge dark shape lunged at him.

Wystan had watched the scene unfold before him with an open mouth, although you might not have noticed that, unless you were looking really quite closely. (Mrs Darling had given him a towel to dry himself off, because she wasn't an unfeeling security guard, and he'd rubbed his beard vigorously and now it was bushy and prickly and sticking out all over the place.)

He'd had time to look around the arena while the Admiral had been talking with his captor. He'd seen Fish lying fast asleep on the pool edge beside the Admiral, and he'd seen the dark shape that he knew was the beeping crocodile floating log-like in the water (and by 'beeping crocodile' I don't mean '*bad word that I'm not writing down* crocodile', I mean 'crocodile that from time to time has been heard to beep').

He'd watched Mrs Darling lock the door, leaving him in the arena with the Admiral, as she went off to continue the hunt for Fizzlebert, and then he'd turned to face the Admiral and gulped as the man had gestured with his metal hook. The big lights that illuminated the pool glinted wickedly off it and Wystan felt like the game was up. He'd looked around the stadium of seating he was stood in and saw no other exit beside the door they'd come in through, other than through the curtain at the back of the stage. He was cut off from the pool itself by a plastic screen, which stopped the audience getting wet during the more lively parts of the show. With his acrobatic prowess he could easily have jumped it, but the soft landing in the water didn't appeal, not when he remembered those pink teeth opening before him. At the opposite end of the seats was a little metal gate that opened onto the pool-edge and it was towards that Admiral Spratt-Haddock was pointing. To Wystan's mind he looked half angry and

half delighted, a dark grin curving across his face, pointing his chin out even further, and then . . .

. . . then a shape burst out past the nautical man, flew through the curtains which flicked and waved like great red wings, and Wystan saw it was a flying Fizz.

'Watch out!' he shouted as his friend got caught, by accident it seemed, on the Admiral's hook, and dangled for a moment before plunging straight down into the water. Admiral Spratt-Haddock wobbled on the edge himself, Fizz's Ringmaster's coat unbalancing him, but he stamped a boot, held out his other arm like a tightrope walker's pole, and stood firm. He leaned over the water and peered down into the bubbles.

Wystan ran along the front row of chairs,

towards the gate that led to the tiled area at the edge of the pool. He didn't understand exactly what Fizz's plan was, how diving in the water was meant to help them escape, but he reckoned getting closer to where Fizz was would be a good start. Get the boys together again, that had to be a step forward, yes?

When he had his hand on the gate he stopped, because something was happening in the water. He could make out the troubled surface, underneath which Fizz was trying to swim, and he could see a dark shape deep down hurtling towards him.

For a moment he couldn't think what it was, then he heard a strange submerged bubbling beeping – *beep beep beep, beep beep beep* – and then he realised what had vanished silently from the surface of the pool. The log-shaped monster, that giant toothy antelope-snatching killer . . .

Then, there was Fizz on the surface of the water, but he was floating face down, his red hair plastered round his head and his arms weakly flapping. Wystan shouted his name as a great dark shape rose beside him, and shouted it again as those heavy jaws opened, water pouring off them.

'No, you wretched beast, you interfering dinosaur,' shouted Spratt-Haddock, waving Fizz's coat at the crocodile.

The noise of those jaws slamming shut was like the thudding stone doors of some dank mausoleum. It sent an electric shock up Wystan's back, and slivers of ice all through his veins. He covered his face with his beard, not wanting to see what had happened to his friend, but his left eye saw everything, because of the hole the shark had bitten.

The crocodile sank beneath the water, and Fizz vanished with it, sucked down in a froth of bubbles.

And then . . .

. . . the crocodile burst up out of the water, balancing Fizz, not between its jaws as Wystan feared, but on the tip of its snout. It pushed him up, out of the water and dumped him down on the concrete, just at the Admiral's feet and then, like a particularly ugly ballerina, it spun and sunk back under the water, snapping its jaws twice.

Recovering his wits from where he'd dropped them, Wystan opened the gate and ran round the pool to where the Admiral was

stood looking down at the unusually deliv-
ered boy.

'Urgh, argh, splurr,' said Fizzlebert, leaning over
the edge of the pool and coughing up water.

He opened his eyes and saw Wystan kneeling beside him.

'I've come to rescue you,' Fizz said weakly.

'What?'

Fizz shook his head. A goldfish fell out of his ear. He looked at Wystan again.

'Wystan,' he said. 'I dreamt I fell in the water.'

'Um, Fizz,' Wystan said, 'you *did* fall in the water. So did I.'

'Oh,' said Fizz.

It was all coming back to him, the conversation he'd overheard, the search for Fish, the chase along the walkways, the sight of the metal hook before his face, the little purple fish like pipe-cleaners. It all came back in a rush, though not in the right order.

'Where's that pirate?' Fizz said, getting to his feet.

'Here,' said a cold voice from behind him. 'And I ain't no pirate, me lad.'

Fizz looked round and indeed, there was

the Admiral, his stupid hat on his head and no beard at all on his big chin. Fizz's red Ringmasterly coat swayed on the tip of his hook. It looked big and warm and dry.

'I'll have that,' Fizz said, snatching it away and struggling to pull it on over his soggy, cold clothes.

'So, *Admiral*, we meet at last,' he said. (That was how, in all the best adventure books he'd read, the hero always greeted the villain.)

Admiral Spratt-Haddock chuckled cruelly at this. Maybe he hadn't read the same books as Fizz had. In the books he would have said something sarcastic.

'Let's cut to the chase. We came here tonight, risking life and limb in the cause of friendship, because you, Admiral, have got Fish.'

The nautical gentleman looked at Fizzlebert and stroked his chin.

'This is a *'Quarium*, me lad. Of course we has fish.'

'No, no, no,' Fizz said, shaking his head. 'I mean you've *stolen* Fish.'

'Oh, the calumny,' the Admiral moaned, looking up to the black night sky and waving his hand. 'How can you stand there and say that, when it's *you*, you circus rat, *you*, you travelling sneak, who's broken into *my* 'Quarium and been off with *my* fish! And we's caught you *red-handed*!'

'I haven't stolen anything!' Fizz shouted, surprised at the Admiral's gale force outburst.

'Well, *someone* has,' the Admiral snapped angrily.

'Who'd want to steal fish?' Fizz demanded.

'A cat burglar?' Wystan suggested, since Unnecessary Sid wasn't there to say it.

The Admiral frowned as if he didn't get the joke (which, to be fair, was easy enough to miss).

'No, *you've* kidnapped Fish, *our*—' Fizz said, getting back to the point.

'*Kidnapped?* Me? *You're* the kidnapper,' blared the Admiral. He prodded Fizz with a pointy flesh and blood finger, and loomed at him, peering face to face, his warm breath and his large chin filling Fizz's view. 'And I'll have you keel-hauled before dawn if you don't tell me what's become of 'em. Me lovely fishes, and you . . . *you* . . .'

'Just tell us what you did with our sea lion!' Fizz shouted.

'Sea lion?'

'Yeah, our sea lion. He's called Fish. And you've stolen him. Kidnapped him.'

'What?'

'It's no good lying, Admiral Spratt-Haddock. We saw him, here, with you, in your show this afternoon.'

'Fish, you say?'

'And, Fizz,' Wystan added excitedly, tugging his friend's sleeve, 'he was here before, when you fell in.' He pointed at the patch of concrete the sea lion had been lying on. 'But when the crocodile saved you . . .'

'What? The crocodile rescued me?' Fizz felt a shiver of fear run down his spine.

'Aye,' the Admiral said thoughtfully. 'I ain't never seen her do something like that before. She don't normally like anyone but me.' He had a strange look on his strange face. It was hard to spot unless you knew what you were looking for (*you'd* never have spotted it if I hadn't pointed it out to you, for instance). It was a puzzled look, a slightly relieved look, a look of hope, perhaps. 'Blasted nuisance, that beast. Followed me from the Nile all the way back to England. Hasn't never hardly let me out of her sight.'

'Why ain't she eaten you?' Wystan said. 'Isn't that what they normally do?'

'You'd think, wouldn't you? But she just likes me company. I was there when her egg hatched, and she saw me and I reckons her little brain said *Mummy!*'

'Really?' asked Fizzlebert, putting the argument they'd been having to one side for a moment, since this was quite interesting, after all.

'Maybe,' the Admiral said with a sigh. 'It's hard to tell with crocodiles. I don't know.'

He shook his head and the soft look that had settled on his face slid off, uncovering the scowl that he'd been wearing before. He slid his hook into the lapel of Fizz's coat and pulled him close.

'Now what's this you're saying about me sea lion, me lad?'

'Fish,' said Fizz. 'Fish is *our* sea lion and we want him back.'

He looked around, scanning the pool and the poolside but couldn't see him anywhere.

'Hang on, lubbers,' the Admiral said. 'You don't mean Pescado?'

'He's called Fish and he belongs to us,' Wystan said.

'Well, he doesn't really *belong* to us,' added Fizz, 'but he's our friend.'

'Yeah,' Wystan went on. 'He lives with us and I do an act with him and now he's gone missing and I saw you at the circus last night and then we saw him here in your show.'

'Hang on, hang on,' said the Admiral, waving his vicious-looking hook to encourage silence. Then he called, 'Pescado! *Pescado!* Where've you got to, you scurvy old lion, you?'

'Not Pescado, *Fish!*'

As Fizz said that, the sea lion slid up out of the water and landed, without a splash or a slosh, on the concrete stage. He barked once, shook water off his head and waddled over to where the Admiral and the boys stood.

'Gentlemen, meet Pescado.'

The sea lion lifted one of its flippers up as if to shake hands and moved its head from

side to side, looking at each boy in turn with
its big deep black eyes.

Fizz and Wystan both stepped forwards,
and Fizz's heart sank. He looked at
Wystan and saw they were thinking the same
thing.

'That's not Fish.'

Dr Surprise had been right. There was
something wrong with his whiskers. Not

wrong, they were perfectly good whiskers, good for whatever whiskers are good for, but they simply weren't Fish's whiskers. It was obvious when you saw them up close.

'Um,' said Fizz, feeling incredibly small and embarrassed. Wystan was hiding behind his beard, but Fizz had nowhere to conceal his embarrassment, so he tried to get rid of it with an apology. 'Sorry,' he mumbled.

'Never mind that, lad. I've been 'ccused of a lot worse in my time . . .'

He sounded like he was going to go on and say more, maybe tell them some of the other things he had been accused of, but he was interrupted.

'Admiral! Admiral!'

It was Mrs Darling. She was waving from the other side of the pool.

'Yes?' called Admiral Spratt-Haddock.

'Oh!' she shouted, seeing Fizz. 'You caught the other one? Well done, sir. But you're too late. You've got to come see what they've done. There's more fish gone, Admiral. You hold them there. I'll get my gloves on, then we can search them. See if we can find what they've nicked.'

'Ah, Mrs Darling,' the Admiral began, but before he could finish his sentence the chapter came to an end.

CHAPTER TWELVE

**In which a crime scene is investigated
and in which the Aquarium is left**

'**M**rs Darling,' the Admiral repeated, for the benefit of anyone who forgot what he'd said at the end of the previous chapter. 'I'm thinking that won't be needed.' (He meant searching the boys.)

'But we caught them . . .'

'Ah, yes, but I don't think *these* are our thieves. I've listened to their yarn, and it's just

been a misunderstanding. They thought *we* were the thundering thieves.'

'But the robberies?'

'Someone else. You're still on the case, Mrs Darling. The game is still afoot.'

'Admiral Spratt-Haddock,' Fizz said, raising his hand in the air.

'Aye, lad?'

'We saw someone.'

The two boys explained to the Admiral and his guard what it was they'd seen: the masked man and his wriggling coat.

'Where was that?' Spratt-Haddock asked.

'In the green room,' Mrs Darling said.

Fizz nodded in agreement.

'You've got to come look,' she said. 'See what he's taken this time.'

* * *

Admiral Spratt-Haddock tapped on the glass with his hook and peered into the water.

'Gone,' he whispered.

There were several empty tanks in the corridor. The one he was stood in front of now had a sign by its side that read GREEN-GILLED MUDSHARK. The tank to the side of that, which he'd looked in first and for a long time, was labelled LESSER GREEN-FOOTED CORAL OCTOPUS. Wystan and Fizz remembered it looking exactly as empty as it did now when they'd seen it that morning and Dr Surprise had been very impressed by its alleged contents, but the Admiral assured them it was *really* empty now and he seemed upset by it.

'But how did he steal it?' Fizz asked, pointing at the mudshark tank. The glass was

208

unbroken. Unless the thief had magic powers, he couldn't have just reached into the water and taken the fish.

'I don't know,' Mrs Darling said. 'I've not been able to work it out. Nothing's ever broken, the doors are all still locked. It's a mystery.'

Fizz had spent long enough in the circus, and especially with Dr Surprise, to know that when things looked impossible, there was usually a perfectly sensible explanation behind them. It had to be the same here.

He looked in the empty tank. He tapped on the glass. He looked at the damp floor where the burglar had been stood when they'd first seen him, wrestling something into the inside pocket of his coat, presumably this mudshark. He looked at all these things in

just the way a detective in a book would, but none of them gave him a clue. None of them leapt out at him shouting, 'Aha! It's me!'

'I don't know,' he said finally. 'I'm stumped.'

'You're Stump,' corrected Wystan.

Fizz raised his eyes to the ceiling at the terrible joke, and saw something that made him think, 'Aha!' after all.

'Look at that,' he said, pointing up.

It was a ceiling tile, like the ones in Mrs Darling's office, and it was slightly askew.

'We surprised him, like you surprised us,' he said to the security guard. 'He didn't have time to put it back straight.'

'But?' she said, taking her hat off and running a hand through her short hair.

'I bet there's no lid on the tank, is there?'

'No,' said the Admiral. 'I likes to give them fishes of mine a dash of the fresh air, like they'd have out at sea.'

'Well, then,' said Fizz. 'He must've had a bendy net or something and poked it up and over the side, through the hole in the ceiling and down into the tank. Then he could watch through the glass as he scooped his fish up.'

'I reckons you're right, lad! But that don't

get us no closer to running the roach rustler to ground.'

'Hang on,' Wystan said, stroking his beard (which is how you can tell a person with a beard has been thinking about something). 'In the office there was a telly screen.'

'Yes,' Mrs Darling said. 'It's linked to all the security cameras.'

'So how come you've not caught the burglar yet?'

'He's quick,' she said, glumly. 'He's crafty. He covers the cameras up. Look over there.'

She pointed to the corner of the corridor, where up on the wall a camera was pointing at them. A little red light blinked, but the lens of the camera had been blocked up with something. All she'd see in her little room was blackness.

Fizzlebert's brain was ticking over. He'd solved mysteries before. Hadn't he saved the circus from Wystan's wicked step-mother? (Yes.) Hadn't he escaped from Mrs Stinkthrottle's house? (Yes.) Well, surely he could solve this mystery now. All he needed was a dead good clue and this might be it.

'Wystan,' he said, 'can you reach the camera? Get whatever it is that's blocking the picture?'

'Sure,' said Wystan.

In one bound and a bounce (using his acrobatic elasticity) he jumped up and snatched the bit of paper that was wedged into the front of the camera.

Fizzlebert unfolded it, half hoping the thief would have used an old envelope with his name and address on. He smoothed it out on the concrete floor and looked at what it was.

'It's just some rubbish, just a bit of random litter,' Mrs Darling said. 'That's no good. It doesn't tell us anything.'

Fizzlebert's brain sparkled inside his head (had the lights been turned out it's possible you might have seen a glow from inside his ear). 'No, no, it does,' he said. 'It tells us a lot. Look at it. It's the wrapper to a packet of flour.'

'So, what does that tell us?' the Admiral said. 'That the sea-sickening villain is a baker?'

'No,' Fizz said. 'Not that. Not quite.'

Beep beep beep. Beep beep beep.

As the sound echoed between fish tanks they stood in silence and watched the great swaggering brute of a crocodile lurch round the corner, glance at the four of them with its flashing amber eyes, lumber over to the Admiral and flop with a scaly crash down at his feet.

Admiral Spratt-Haddock sighed, and rolled his eyes in embarrassment.

The crocodile yawned hugely, revealing long rows of large yellow teeth and a vast pink tongue.

'Wow,' Wystan said. 'Imagine sticking your head in there, Fizz.'

Fizz tried not to, though now it had been mentioned it was hard to shake the idea.

'Ignore her,' Admiral Spratt-Haddock said as the crocodile rubbed its head on his boot and lay down to snore gently. 'She's harmless. Wouldn't hurt a fly. Take the leg off an antelope, mind you, but the flies'd be fine.' He scratched his chin. 'You were saying, me lad, something about that bit of paper. A clue, d'ya reckon?'

'Oh yes,' said Fizz, stepping away from the crocodile. 'I think . . . I think I've got it all worked out. We need to get back to the circus.'

'The circus,' said the Admiral, excitedly. 'I *knew* this was the squid-juggling circus's fault!'

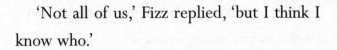

'Not all of us,' Fizz replied, 'but I think I know who.'

On their way to the front doors they went past a tank at the end of the pink corridor. Wystan stopped and looked into it.

'I think this is the one I fell in,' he said.

'Yes, sorry about that,' the Admiral said. 'It's supposed to have a lid on, that one.'

As Fizz looked into the water a dark pink shape (a shark-shaped dark pink shape, mind you) loomed up from between some weeds. He jumped at the sight, but Wystan leant in even closer.

'She's not so big,' he said.

'She's a he,' the Admiral corrected, 'and he's only young.'

'Was Wystan in danger?'

'Oh no, this is an Austrian Blushing Shark. Very shy. Mostly vegetarians.'

The shark still had a few strands of scraggly black hair caught between his teeth.

'It's a hair-bevore,' Fizz said, slapping his bearded pal on the back. (Unnecessary Sid would've been very proud of that joke.)

Wystan felt the hole in his beard and grumbled, 'I did have hair before, so you can say that again.'

But Fizz didn't say it again. He thought, quite rightly, that for some jokes, once is more than enough.

Mrs Darling locked the glass doors behind them as the Admiral and the two boys stepped out into the cool of the evening. She was staying behind, because a guard's work, as she said, is, so long as there is something left to guard, guarding.

As the Admiral and the boys walked along the prom, into the night, the sea, which was off to their right, down in the dark, roared and sloshed up and down the beach. The salt spray sang in their nostrils and Fizz was reminded of what he'd almost forgotten in the excitement of the hunt for the fish burglar.

'I wish we'd found Fish,' he said to the Admiral. 'I really thought you had him. We were certain.'

The evening was cool, and he felt even colder in his dripping clothes. He was leaving damp footprints behind him. With every step his shoes squeaked, his socks squirted water up his ankles and his trousers *shthwacked* together.

'I dunno,' Wystan said, wringing a few more drops of water out of his beard. 'If he don't turn up, what am I gonna do? I ain't got no act without Fish.'

Fizz didn't say anything to that. He knew, even when they did find Fish, that *he* didn't have an act come tomorrow, not unless Captain Fox-Dingle had found a miracle cure for old age, and since he wasn't a doctor and miracles are hard to come by, that seemed unlikely.

'The sea lion,' the Admiral intoned in his deepest, most wise tones, 'is a mysterious creature. The sea lion is his own master, we merely borrow his attention for a time. Pescado came to me, me lads, in me hour of need. He just rocked up one evening and brought his act to my 'Quarium. One day, I know, he will wander off, flollop down the beach and be gone, off into the great sea to find himself a new destiny. And maybe, just maybe, this Fish of yours is the same. Maybe he's heard the call of the ocean singing in his salty veins. Maybe he has been called home.'

Fizz hoped what the Admiral was saying wasn't true, that Fish hadn't grown tired of travelling round with the circus. They shouldn't have come to the seaside at all, not if one whiff of the salt breeze could tempt his friend away. He blamed the Ringmaster, he blamed Bill, the head lorry driver who drove the truck with the Big Top on, he blamed anyone he could, except Fish.

Fizz missed him something rotten at that moment. He wondered if he'd ever see his kipper-flavoured friend again.

Ahead of them they could see the lights of the circus through the row of trees that separated the park from the prom, and when the wind whipped round in their direction they could hear the muted sound of music coming from the Big Top. The evening's show wasn't over yet. With any luck the boys wouldn't even have been missed.

Now, Fizz told himself, was not a time to be sad. There was work to be done. And when there's work to be done, the best thing to do is to do it. He knew exactly where he could find the Admiral's nemesis, the burglar, the thief, the robber.

'Come on,' he said, 'Even if we've not found Fish, maybe we can rescue some fish of yours.' And with that he ran straight into the next chapter.

CHAPTER THIRTEEN

**In which fish are found and in which
a villain is faced**

'**F**izz!'

Captain Fox-Dingle had spotted them sneaking into the circus and was shouting from the steps of his caravan.

He looked miserable. His moustache, small as it was, seemed to be drooping uncombed and unkempt across his top lip.

The show was going on in the Big Top (they

could hear the audience applauding and laughing and the band playing) and the Captain was having to miss it all. No wonder he looked sad. And then he caught sight of who Fizzlebert was with.

He stepped off the bottom step, just as the trio of potential heroes came to a stop.

Captain Fox-Dingle looked at the Admiral. He looked at his dark sailor's coat, at his rather appropriate nautical hat, at the hook on his hand. Took the whole lot in in one slow sweeping look from head to toe.

'Fizz?' he asked.

'It's all right Captain,' Fizz said hurriedly. 'He's from the Aquarium, we're helping him find his lost fish.'

'Admiral Spratt-Haddock,' the Admiral said holding his hand out to shake (not his hook-hand, but his hand-hand). 'Delighted to meet a fellow—'

Captain Fox-Dingle interrupted, ignoring Spratt-Haddock's words and hand and speaking to Fizz instead.

'Come.'

And with that he turned on his heel and strode off behind his caravan, assuming that the boys would follow.

'I'm sorry about that, Admiral,' Fizz said. 'He's got a lot on his mind at the moment.'

The Admiral shook his head. 'Not everyone's got the knack of making shipmates, Fizz,' he said.

'But he didn't need to be so rude. He's a lion-tamer, you're a fish-tamer: I reckoned you'd be friends.'

'It don't work like that, Fizzlebert. Things

ain't always as simple as they should be. Look at the rest of tonight. You thought you'd just come along to the 'Quarium and find your sea lion, but that didn't happen, did it? Instead we're hunting a fish-napper—'

'Speaking of which,' Wystan interrupted, 'shouldn't we be . . .'

'Yes,' Fizz said resolutely. 'We've got a thief to catch.'

'But what about the Captain? He wanted you to go with him,' Admiral Spratt-Haddock said. 'I don't want to get you in trouble, boys.'

Fizz was torn. He could guess where the Captain had gone. Round the back of the caravan was where Charles's cage was. He wanted to see the lion, but at the same time he wanted to follow his plan and finish his mission. The longer he waited the more likely it was the Admiral's fish might be cooked.

The trio crept through the circus, passing caravans and tents and wagons and trucks. The Admiral drew odd looks from some lounging riggers, but when they saw he was with Fizz they tipped their hats and said 'Good evening,' and went back to their conversations. Other than that they were undisturbed as they made their way to the large tent where Fizz thought the answer to the mystery of the missing fish would be uncovered.

'Are you sure about this?' Wystan whispered as Fizz lifted the flap and poked his head in.

'As sure as custard's hot,' Fizz said, confidently.

'But custard's not always—'

'Shhh,' added Fizz before Wystan could finish pointing things out.

The Mess Tent was empty, the lights were out. They tiptoed towards the serving bench where Cook dished up the evening meal. There was a light coming from back there, from behind the bench where the kitchen tent joined onto the Mess Tent. That was where Fizz thought they'd find their culprit.

'Oh!' said Admiral Spratt-Haddock, as they got closer. It was an 'Oh!' of shock, and when Fizz looked at what the Admiral was looking at he understood why.

There on the blackboard was chalked the menu from earlier that evening.

COD & CHIPS & SEAWEED

Underneath it said: VEGETARIAN OPTION: CHIPS & SEAWEED

The Admiral touched the writing with the curve of his hook. 'Craddock,' he said.

'Who?' said Wystan.

'Craddock the Choral Cod,' Fizz said. 'Remember this morning at the Admiral's show? He said Craddock had gone missing. I was too busy thinking about Fish to pay much attention, but then this evening when we had our tea,' (he pointed at the board) 'I remembered it. The cod and chips reminded me of it, but I didn't for one minute think I was eating *that* cod.'

'We ate the Admiral's fish?'

'I reckon so. We've been having an awful lot of fish this last week, haven't we?'

'What did you have yesterday, me lad?' asked Spratt-Haddock, a slight tremble in his voice.

Fizz tried to remember. He'd been eating it when Cook and Fish had their argument. No! That wasn't quite true, was it? He'd been pushing it around his plate because he didn't want to eat it. It had reminded him of his mum . . . it was fricasséed clown fish.

He told the Admiral, and could tell, when he didn't get a reply, that the clown fish must've gone missing the night before.

Between the Mess Tent and kitchen was a thin canvas curtain, which could be tied up when the place was in use, but which was hanging down now. There was a light on behind it, and like a shadow puppet show they could see the silhouette of someone moving about in there. It would have been a pretty rubbish shadow puppet show, since the image was faint and kept moving out of the way of

230

the light and vanishing, but all the same it told one simple story, which was all that Fizz needed to know: there was someone at home.

'Do we just burst in, or what?' he asked the Admiral.

'Oh I think so, don't you?' said Admiral Spratt-Haddock patting his belt, where a cutlass would have been had he been a pirate (which he wasn't).

'Drop your fish and put your hands in the air!' shouted Admiral Spratt-Haddock as he leapt through the curtains into the kitchen.

He stood, his hands on his hips, a determined, steely look on his big chin. A breeze came from somewhere and rippled his coat. He looked every inch a nautical man in control.

'Oh dear!' squeaked Dr Surprise, surprised.

'Dr Surprise?' said Fizz, looking around the kitchen. 'What are you doing here?'

'I was just getting a glass of milk for Flopples,' the Doctor said in a tremulous tone, holding a glass of milk in the air and pointing at it. 'She always likes a warm glass of milk after the show, it helps her relax.'

'Where's Cook?' asked Wystan.

'Who's Flopples?' asked the Admiral, at the same time.

'Pardon?' said Dr Surprise to both of them, having heard neither.

'After you,' said the Admiral to Wystan.

'Dr Surprise,' mumbled the boy through his beard, the wind having been taken from the sails of his expostulation, 'have you seen Cook anywhere?'

'Cook?' said the Doctor. 'Now let me think.'

He took a sip of the milk he was holding in his hand, realised he didn't like milk, pulled a face and said, 'He *was* just here. I think he's popped out to the freezers.' He pointed to the flap that led to the smaller tent with the freezers in. Fizz could hear the faint rumble of the generator that kept them cold.

'He's stolen the Admiral's fish, Dr

 233

Surprise,' said Fizz. 'You've got to help us stop him.'

'Fish?'

'From the 'Quarium, Doctor. Fizzlebert here reckons your Cook's the one what's been breaking in, robbing me fish and serving them up for your dinner.'

'Oh, surely not?'

'It all fits, Dr Surprise. All the fish dinners we've had this last week, and we found an empty packet of flour at the Aquarium, and Cook's the only one round here who'd have flour packets, and we had cod for tea tonight, didn't we? Battered cod, and Craddock was missing from the show this morning, do you remember?'

'Well, yes, I suppose, but it's probably a coincidence, Fizz.'

'I wondered about that, but then I

remembered what you'd said this morning. When we were talking about Fish, you told me who Cook's dad was. You said he was the son of Terry Trapp the escapologist. And that explains why no one could work out how the break-ins had been done. No one's better with unlocking locked locks than an escapologist, and I bet his dad taught him all the tricks of the act, don't you?'

'But *why*, Fizz? I mean, why break into an Aquarium to steal fish?'

'It's probably the best place to get them,' said Wystan.

'Well, it all sounds rather silly to me.' The Doctor dismissed the idea with a wave of his glass of milk.

'But we *saw* him,' Fizz said loudly, stamping his foot.

'You *saw* him?' The Doctor put the glass of milk down. He screwed his monocle tightly into his eye socket and peered closer at the three of them.

'Yeah, when we were in the Aquarium looking for Fish.'

'When you were looking for fish? I thought you said Cook was stealing the fish?'

'No, Doctor, we were looking for *Fish*, and while we were there we bumped into the burglar, only we didn't know who it was at the time. But . . .'

Fizz stopped talking.

'What is it, Fizz?' asked Wystan.

'I've just thought of something. We didn't know who *he* was, not then, but he saw us too. And he just ran off and left us there, in the Aquarium, at the scene of the crime. He left us to get caught in his place while he ran.'

'He did what?' said Dr Surprise, suddenly standing straight, and looking very angry. His moustache wobbled violently. His monocle glittered. 'How dare he, Fizzlebert? How very dare he? You wait here. If what you say is true, I'll feed him to Flopples.'

'Who *is* this Flopples?' asked the Admiral, not having had an answer earlier.

'My rabbit,' said the Doctor.

'Of course she is,' said the Admiral.

Dr Surprise pulled his pocket watch out of his waistcoat pocket (he'd been to the watch-mender's that afternoon and picked it up). It swung in the air before him, shiny and newly polished, without a rabbit tooth-mark in sight. It glinted gloriously in the

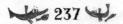

sharp kitchen lights, sparkling and twirling and ticking loudly.

'Stay here,' he said.

He sounded stern. Fizz wanted to do as he was told. He wasn't sure he knew why he wanted to do as he was told, but he did. He stayed where he was. So did Wystan and the Admiral.

They looked at each other from the corners of their eyes.

The Doctor walked toward the flapway (which is a new word I've just invented to describe a doorway in a tent) he'd pointed at a minute earlier.

He stepped through it.

Then nothing happened.

A moment later, from a different flapway, Cook walked into the kitchen, chewing his

stubby pencil between his teeth, humming to himself and holding a large carrot.

'Here you go,' he said, before looking up.

He stopped when he saw the boys.

He stopped even more when he saw the Admiral.

He said something that Fizz thought was a swearword, although it was new to him and he knew he'd have to check it in a big dictionary next time he visited a library.

Then Cook said, 'You again. How'd you get back here? And what's *he* doing here?' He pointed at the Admiral, with the carrot (which oddly made it an even more threatening gesture than normal). 'What's going on?'

Fizz wanted to say, 'Aha! We've caught you, you thief. We know what you've been up to, but the game's over now. Just give yourself

up and we'll call the police and you can be arrested, which is what should happen to all criminals, but first show us what you've done with the fish you stole this evening. Are they still alive?'

But what he actually said was, '—'

He tried to move his mouth, but he couldn't. It was as if his mouth didn't want to work. His brain was happily working away, but his mouth, no. He tried to move his hands to touch his mouth, see what was wrong, but he found his whole body was frozen. Not frozen as in cold, but frozen as in unmoving. However hard he thought, his body simply refused to follow his orders.

'Nothing to say, eh?' jeered Cook. He scratched his stubble with the carrot. 'Not so brave now, are you? Think you're so brilliant,

always sticking your head in that fleabag's gob. As if *that's* anything special, just 'cause Mr and Mrs Stump want their son to be a star. And you, Beardy, you're just as bad with your greedy thieving flolloping sea lion. You all think you're so much *better* than old Cook, don't you?'

While Fizz was listening to this rant his brain was whirring. He realised what had happened, why he and the others were frozen in place. They'd made the mistake of looking at Dr Surprise's watch when he pulled it out. It had swayed, just like it did in his show when he'd get someone from the audience and hypnotise them. And as they'd looked at it, what was it the Doctor had said? 'Stay there.'

The problem with Dr Surprise was, he didn't realise his own power. And now he'd

left them trapped with this, it was becoming increasingly clear, madman. Fizz hoped the Doctor would be back soon.

'Without *me*,' Cook was going on, 'this circus would be *nothing*. But no one thinks about that do they? No one puts *Cook's* name on the posters. No one shouts *Cook's* name in the Big Top, do they? No. They say, "Hey Cook, we're *hungry*." They say, "Hey Cook, we're waiting for our *dinner*." They say, "Hey Cook, can I have some *more?*" Cook! Cook! Cook! That's all I hear.' He put the carrot down and picked up a meat cleaver (which is a sort of knife with a massive square blade, specially made for whacking off great hunks of meat and careless fingers). 'Do you know what, though? That's – Not – My – Name!'

With each word he slammed the huge

knife down on the chopping board, sending chunks of carrot flying through the air.

He stepped towards the three of them, waving the hunk of sharpened metal in his hand. It dripped with orange carrot juice. Fizz looked to his side, with his eyes, and saw the Admiral looking back at him. There was a bead of sweat trickling down the side of his face, as if he were really trying his hardest to move.

'*You*,' Cook shouted, waving the chopper in Admiral Spratt-Haddock's face. 'You were a dream come true, weren't you, with your *seafood supermarket* just up the prom. The Ringmaster's always on at me to cut costs, to keep the expenses down. But it's not just that, oh no. You see, I know *who* you are, Admiral Fish-Brains. You're another one of them *animal trainers.*' Cook spat at the ground, as if the words disgusted him. 'There's loads of your sort round here. Trembly with all her lovely horses, prancing around with their feathery headdresses. Erasmus Dockery and his Educated Iguanas. Dingle, with his mangy old lion. Oh, I remember when he turned up, when the Ringmaster made the announcement. Coming in, stealing the show, stealing the limelight. "We've got a lion act now," they said, "no need for Terry Trapp's boy." Criminal! That's what it was. Criminal!'

Fizz could see hear the swish of the meat chopper as Cook waved it around underneath the Admiral's nose, chopping the air into small slivers. If Admiral Spratt-Haddock had had a moustache, it would have been all gone by now, Cook was waving it that close.

'Well, it was my *pleasure* to ruin your rotten fish house, just as it's my *pleasure* to supply Dingle's rotten meat. Hah! *Anything* to make the *zookeepers* unhappy.' He chuckled, to himself, wickedly. His red eyes flared. 'When that lion's gone, they'll come begging me. They'll be on their knees. "Oh," they'll say, "Terry Trapp's boy, will you come and do your act for us?" Then it'll be no more cooking! No more chopping and roasting and toasting! That'll be tomorrow, but today . . .'

He stopped talking and looked around. He scratched his ear with the cleaver, then he turned back. Fizz still couldn't move. He tried shouting, but nothing came out.

'Today, though, I've got a problem, ain't I? You three know too much. So, I'm going to have to do something about it. I think a

mysterious disappearance, don't you? That'll put an end to all this fish on the menu. No more complaints. I'll give 'em meat pies. Tell 'em they're pork pies, eh? No one'll know the difference.'

Fizz wanted to gulp. Could Cook really mean it? Surely not. But when Fizz looked in his eyes, as bloodshot and red as they usually were, he was sure the bloke had gone potty. They were flashing with lightning and creased round with anger. This was exactly the moment Dr Surprise should come back, he thought. A click of his fingers and the three of them would be free, and they'd be able to jump on Cook and pin him down.

Except he hadn't come back.

Fizz tried extra hard to move . He concentrated and strained and wished and . . .

. . . his finger, the little one on his left hand, moved half a centimetre.

It was a start.

A very small start.

'Okay, we'll start with the big one!' shouted Cook, pulling the Admiral forwards.

Fizz saw him lift the cleaver high and then he heard a noise.

If he'd been able to turn his head, he would've turned to look at where it came from. He wasn't able to, but Cook was, and he looked round, understandably anxious to not be disturbed in his chopping.

Beep beep beep. Beep beep beep.

Through the side of the tent a dark shape lunged, so huge and fast it burst the canvas into ribbons, its clawed feet propelling it forwards like a scaly missile.

248

'Arrghhh!' screamed Cook, never having been attacked by a huge crocodile before, and, apparently, not being open to new experiences.

He fell backwards, knocking saucepans off work surfaces, and dropping his meat cleaver onto the grass at their feet. There was an awful clattering and crashing and the man fell out of sight, behind benches and tables, with the crocodile following him.

Fizz couldn't see what was going on, but he could hear. Cook was shouting, which meant at least he hadn't been eaten yet. Things were falling over. It was a cacophony.

And then it wasn't. One word had cut through the noise and turned it to silence.

'Sit!'

Well, almost silence. Fizz could hear Cook

babbling in fear, somewhere on the floor out of sight.

'Naughty,' said Captain Fox-Dingle, from the side of the tent.

The Captain was wagging his finger and telling the crocodile off. And to Fizz's amazement, the crocodile was listening.

'He's not out there. And he's not in his caravan. I went and checked. We ought to tell the Ringmaster. He must be found. I wonder if—' said Dr Surprise, coming into the tent through the flapway he'd gone out five minutes before. He stopped when he saw the wreckage all around him. 'Um?' he said.

'Croc,' said Captain Fox-Dingle, pointing at the huge reptile.

'Oh yes. Oh my,' said the Doctor. 'And *there's* Cook,' he added, pointing underneath

the crocodile. 'Croc and the cook. Cook and the croc.' He looked at the boys, and at the Admiral. 'Why are you all standing there?'

'Mmm-nnn-gghh,' said Fizz, pointing at himself with his little finger.

Dr Surprise still had his watch in his hand, like a gangster might carry a revolver. He looked at it and said, 'Oh. Cripes.' Then he clicked his fingers and Fizz felt every muscle in his body relax.

He was free again.

Somewhere outside he could hear the circus band playing the walkout music, which is what they play at the end of the show after the big finale, for everyone in the audience to, well, walk out to. And he could hear the excited chatter and laughter of a happy audience passing by the Mess Tent on their ways home. If only, he thought, they'd seen the show that had happened in here this evening. They'd really have got their money's worth. *Death-defying* was one way to describe it. (Although only just.)

CHAPTER FOURTEEN

In which ends are tied up and in which the circus moves on

Once he was able, Fizz poured the whole story out.

Captain Fox-Dingle listened, his moustache quivering. Even though he was a military man and notoriously reserved, the idea that Cook had been about to do what he'd been about to do made him go purple in the face. He didn't seem to mind so much about having eaten half of the Admiral's fish.

'Well, lads,' said the Admiral, when Fizz had finished. 'We've got to work out what to do about this.' He pointed at Cook, who was still underneath the crocodile. 'I'm angry about my fish. I could keel-haul the man, I could gut him from gizzard to lizard and leave him for the seagulls, but that's not the point. That won't bring back Craddock and the rest. And you're moving on in the morning, you could take him with you. But I'm worried for you boys. What'll happen to you if he's not . . . dealt with? We're going to have to get the police in.'

'Maybe not,' said Dr Surprise. 'I've got an idea. But first we need to move the, uh . . .'

He pointed at the crocodile.

'Good luck with that,' said Admiral Spratt-Haddock. 'I've been trying to tell her what to do for years. Threw me alarm clock at her once and she *still* follows me around, getting in the way and beeping when she gets excited. She don't do nothing that I say.'

Captain Fox-Dingle twitched his little moustache at that. 'Easy,' he said.

He stepped over and tapped the crocodile on its armour-plated shoulder, and said 'Off,' in a firm voice.

The crocodile opened an amber eye, eyed the Captain for a moment, and then stood up and waddled away to another corner of the tent.

'Oh, Captain Fix-Dongle,' the Admiral said. 'You're a marvel and no mistake.'

'It's Fox-Dingle,' whispered Fizz.

'Is it?' said the Admiral, innocently.

'Sprott-Hiddock,' said Captain Fox-Dingle.

'It's Spratt-Haddock,' said Fizz, before he realised the Captain had just done the unimaginable. He'd cracked a joke. Hadn't he?

The Admiral laughed and clapped the Captain on the back.

'Oh, that's a good one, you old dog!'

Fox-Dingle coughed. One joke was quite

enough and he didn't approve of all this back-slapping and laughter.

'Croc?' he asked, pointing at the beast.

'Yes, indeed, sir,' Admiral Spratt-Haddock said. 'If you're minded to train her, and if she'll stay, then she's yours, Captain. All yours.'

Fox-Dingle rubbed his hands together and his small square moustache perked up.

'Captain,' Fizz said, tugging at his sleeve. 'I've just remembered something else Cook said. He said he'd been giving you Charles's meat. It sounded like he'd been poisoning it or something. So maybe Charles is going to be alright now? Maybe he'll get better?'

As the Captain looked at Fizzlebert there was softness round the edges of his eyes. He shook his head slowly.

'No,' he said.

Which, Fizz realised, meant several things. First it meant Charles wouldn't be getting better, that he *was* old and tired and there's nothing to stop that. But secondly it meant, 'No, I've not been feeding Charles with the scraps Cook gave me, I've been ordering premium steak and great chewing bones from local butchers. I didn't want to hurt Cook's feelings by telling him this.'

Sometimes a simple 'No,' in the right hands says a whole lot more than you might think.

While they'd been talking Dr Surprise had been leaning over Cook. Fizz had noticed some pocket-watch waving and had looked away quickly, not wanting to be zapped by a hypnotic timepiece.

'There we go,' Dr Surprise said, standing up.

Cook stood beside him. His eyes looked much less crazy, less bloodshot than before and underneath his stubble his mouth was curved into something of a smile.

'What I've done,' the Doctor went on, pointing to his watch, 'is, I've removed all memories of this last week, of his burglaries and of this evening's . . . unfortunate events. And, on top of that, I've instructed him to love cooking. From what you said, Fizzlebert, it sounded like he was jealous of everyone in the ring, everyone with an *act*. Well, the answer to that is simple. It is to love what *you* do, not to hate everyone else for what *they* do. So, he's now a chef to his bones. For him, now, every mealtime will be a display of his talents. An act, in fact. Every empty plate will be like a round of applause to his ears. I think we'll see a marked improvement in standards round here.'

'Can you do that?' Fizz asked.

'I have,' the Doctor said.

'I mean, *should* you do that? Is it right?'

'I think he'll be happier now, Fizzlebert,' the Doctor said, which wasn't really an answer, but sometimes the real answer is complicated. 'And this way, we don't need to tell your parents that you *ran away at night and broke into an Aquarium*, and we don't need to tell the Ringmaster any of it. And anything we can do to not worry that fine gentleman, I think, is for the good.'

Fizz didn't know what to say to that, so he just looked at Wystan and then at the

260

Captain and then at the Admiral and said, 'Okay.'

The next morning the sun rose and the birds sang and it didn't rain and all was good and right and proper in the world. All around the circus riggers were deconstructing things and trucks were being loaded up with tents and cages. The Big Top had been taken down in the early hours of the morning.

The circus was getting ready to move on.

Fizz made his way over to Captain Fox-Dingle's place to see how Charles was.

The Captain had polished the buttons on his uniform extra hard. They gleamed in the sunlight, dazzling Fizz as he came near.

'Captain Fox-Dingle,' he said. 'How's Charles?'

The Captain pointed to a truck Fizz didn't recognise. On the side of it were painted the words: TWILIGHT TOPS, and underneath in smaller writing it said: A RED NOSE RETIREMENT HOME.

'Alright mate,' said a burly chap who was about to climb into the lorry's cab. 'You the lad wiv the head?'

Fizz thought for a moment, before understanding what the man meant and nodding.

'Round the back, mate.'

Fizzlebert Stump went to the back of the truck and found that the doors were open. Inside was a cage and inside the cage was Charles. He looked tired. When he saw Fizz he yawned and grumbled a small greeting-ish roar. Fizz reached through the bars and patted his nose.

'Goodbye,' he said, a lump in his throat almost blocking the way up for the word.

He felt a hand on his shoulder.

'He'll be alright, won't he? They'll take care of him, won't they?'

Captain Fox-Dingle said nothing, but he squeezed tightly. Fizz felt that was a good enough answer from the Captain. In fact, because he knew how much the Captain cared about Charles, he hadn't really needed to ask.

'Alright, chums?' the driver said. 'I've got a schedule to keep. Sign here and we'll have old Chaz here up at Twilight Tops in time for lunch.'

Captain Fox-Dingle signed the clipboard and helped the driver to shut the doors.

They watched the truck drive off, slowly

out the park and then it turned away onto the main road and was gone.

Then the Captain turned to Fizz and said, 'New act.'

'What?'

The Captain didn't say anything more, but led Fizz away to the large cage in which Charles had spent his days. In it was the crocodile. She watched them with beady amber eyes and slowly waved her tail. Fizz felt a butterfly bloom in his stomach, because he understood what the Captain meant.

'Kate.'

The tail stopped waving.

'Open.'

The crocodile's jaws slowly parted, wider and wider. The yellowed teeth glistened moistly and the fat pink tongue pulsed like a heart. Fizz looked into the long space between those jaws with a bravery mingled with terror. There was room in there for a boy's head.

Well, he thought, a circus can't stand still, even the best act must move on. This would be a challenge. No false teeth here. As soon as the circus unloaded itself in the next town they could begin practising.

Wow, he thought, coming round to the idea. *This is going to be a brilliant act. Just wait until I tell Wystan!*

And with that thought he remembered what he'd forgotten in all the excitement and sadness.

Fish!

'Sorry Captain,' he said, 'I've got to go see Wystan.'

And Fizz ran across to Miss Tremble's caravan (which was just over the way from the Captain's, so he wasn't even out of breath when he got there).

'Wystan, Wystan!' he shouted.

He banged on the door, and after a moment a startled Miss Tremble answered, clutching her dressing gown tight and holding a large hairbrush in her hand.

'Yes?' she said.

'Excuse me, Miss Tremble,' Fizz said, 'where's Wystan?'

'I think he's round the back, isn't he? Playing with Fish.'

'What?'

'In his paddling pool.'

'What?'

'I just saw them out the window.'

'What?'

Fizz jumped off the steps and ran round her caravan, past the portable horse paddock, right round to where Fish's paddling pool usually sat, and there in the middle of it was Wystan, in a pair of bathing trunks, and Fish, in his spangly waistcoat and a Moroccan fez (which is the sort of hat Fish is wearing in the accompanying picture).

'Fish!' Fizz shouted.

Fish turned to face him, thinking that a person who shouted 'Fish!' might have a fish on them, and let out a haddock-flavoured burp which wafted right into Fizz's face.

'How . . . ?'

'I think,' Wystan said, since Fish wasn't going to answer, 'he's been out in the sea. There was seaweed in his waistcoat and a crab hanging onto a flipper, which makes sense, but where he got the tattoo, poker chip and the cool new hat, I don't know and he ain't telling. But he must've seen the circus getting packed up and I reckon he didn't want to be left behind. So he came home.'

Fish honked as if to say, 'That's right.' But because animals can't talk he was never able to tell anyone exactly where he'd been those last few days, or why he'd decided to come back when he did. Fizz and Wystan just chose to believe what they believed, because it seemed sensible, even if it meant all the grownups kept saying, '*See*, we said he'd come back,' which was astonishingly annoying.

So there it was. The end of their stay by the seaside.

Wystan and Fish had their act back together.

The Captain and Fizz had a new act to rehearse, even scarier than his old one.

Admiral Spratt-Haddock had offloaded an overly friendly crocodile.

And Dr Surprise had reprogrammed Cook's brain so he was a happy and talented chef.

THE END

Except, there's just one last thing I need to tell you, something Fizz didn't see, but which I think may be important to the story. Or it may not be. You decide. Anyway, here it is.

CHAPTER FOURTEEN-AND-A-HALF

In which Flopples makes another
appearance

It was the night before. All the excitement in the kitchen was over. The all-new improved Cook had finished tidying up and was beginning to plan some new recipes for breakfast. Captain Fox-Dingle had wandered off with the crocodile. The boys had gone to bed. All was quiet in the circus.

There was a knock on a caravan door, metal on wood.

There was a creak as the door opened.

In the doorway stood Dr Surprise. Even though it was late, he didn't have a hair out of place, his monocle was bright and clear and his plastic moustache was elegantly placed. His white rabbit, Flopples, was cradled in his arms like a baby. Her nose twitched.

'Yes?' Dr Surprise quavered in his high voice.

'Now, I looked in his freezers,' Admiral Spratt-Haddock said, starting his conversation in the middle rather than at the beginning. 'And I found in there the last fish he stole. Me green-gilled mudsharks. Nothing I can do for them now. But I think he took something else, Doctor.'

As he spoke the Admiral cleaned under his

fingernails with the tip of his hook. His large
navy blue coat fluttered in the gentle breeze
that blew between the caravans and his eyes
had a slightly unnerving gleam about them.

'Oh yes?'

'Me prize mollusc, me extremely rare and
extremely talented lesser green-footed coral
octopus were gone this evening. The tank
were empty. *But*, it ain't in the freezer. And
that's when I thought of you, Doc.'

'Me?'

'I couldn't help but remember the visit
you made last week. You looked at me octopus and you asked how much it would cost to
buy and I said—'

'Oh, much more money than a simple
circus employee could find.'

'It be a very rare octopus, Doctor.'

'And beautiful, Admiral.'

The two men looked at each other. The Doctor stroked Flopples with one hand and the Admiral picked between his teeth with his hook. There was a tense silence.

'I thought,' the Admiral said eventually, 'you might have heard something. Maybe this villainous chef of yours might've offered you an octopus at a knock-down price? Maybe . . . he was even working for—'

'Oh no, no,' said the Doctor, his monocle glinting. 'You shouldn't think such suspicious thoughts, Admiral. They stick in the brain and drive a man mad. That's what happened with Cook, remember, all that jealousy and suspicion? You heard him. His brain needed a good wash. Me, on the other hand, I'm just a simple showman, happy and honest.'

He stroked Flopples under the chin and she twitched her nose and shook her lovely white ears.

'Never liked rabbits myself,' the Admiral muttered, watching with a shudder.

'Goodnight, now,' Dr Surprise said, in a manner that meant, 'This conversation is over, please go away.'

'No,' Admiral Spratt-Haddock snapped, angry at being dismissed. 'I ain't finished, Doc, I still got questions. Before I go, I want to get this cleared up.'

'Of course,' said Doctor Surprise amiably, 'I think I've got time before bed.'

With his free hand he looped his pocket-watch out of his pocket, just to check.

* * *

'Goodnight, Admiral,' Dr Surprise said a minute later. 'Say goodnight, Flopples.'

And as the perfectly satisfied Admiral walked off into the night, humming a happy nautical tune into the dark air, heading back to his slightly diminished but now safe and secure Aquarium, the white rabbit unfurled a long greenish-white tentacle and waved him goodbye.

FIZZLEBERT'S FIRST ADVENTURE...

Fizzlebert Stump lives in a travelling circus. He hangs around with acrobats, plays the fool with clowns, and puts his head in a lion's mouth every night.
But it can be a bit lonely being the only kid in the circus.
So one day, Fizz decides to join a library -
and that's when it all goes terribly wrong ...

A story of a boy, a book, some very bad people,
some very brave deeds,
and the importance of rubber teeth for lions.

ISBN: 9781408830031   £5.99

FIZZLEBERT'S SECOND ADVENTURE . . .

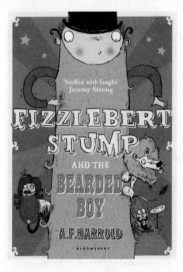

The bearded Barboozul family are the new stars of
Fizzlebert Stump's circus. Their act is full of magic,
mystery, fun and fear. But then things start to go wrong.
The lion loses his dentures. The clowns lose their noses. The
Ringmaster loses his temper. And the circus is about to lose its
licence. Is the bearded boy to blame?

A story of friendship, fiendish schemes,
emergency tuna, and the importance of
proper beard care.

ISBN: 9781408835210   £5.99